I0817827

THE
WINTER
BOYFRIEND

CHRISTINA
BENJAMIN

Published in the United States by Crown Atlantic Publishing

ISBN XXX

Text set in Adobe Garamond

Version 1.1
Printed in the United States of America
First edition hardcover printed, November 2018

To those who never give up on the idea of family.

PROLOGUE

hloe

September 3rd

Dear Journal,
Today is first day of senior year!
I can't wait to see Brady.
This is going to be the best year ever . . .

Chloe Price stood outside the red double doors of Westerly High. She inhaled the crisp fall air. Maple leaves tumbled by in the breeze, carrying with it the faint scent of pumpkin spice, which seemed to be everywhere this time of year. It wouldn't be long until the fall leaves were covered in snow and the smell of pumpkin spice was exchanged for pine wreaths and mistletoe.

Bah humbug, Chloe thought grumpily. She hated Christmas and how it took over her life. Christmas to Chloe meant long hours working at her family business, a chore she didn't look forward to.

The only thing keeping her spirits up was the fact that this would be the last year she had to spend in her tiny, uninteresting corner of the world, working at her family's Christmas tree farm. In a few months she'd be graduating and moving to New York City for college. She couldn't wait to escape upstate New York.

Ever since Chloe's older sister Margot moved to the city, Chloe had been counting the days until she could join her. It's not that Chloe didn't love her parents. She did. They were disgustingly in love and annoyingly involved in her life. But that wasn't the problem. The problem was that they owned and operated a Christmas tree farm and lodge. And for as long as Chloe could remember, she'd been forced to do her family duty and work at the farm as well.

Eighteen years of Christmas as a year-round holiday had made Chloe desperate to escape the small town of Pine Island. The only thing making her slightly less desperate was her boyfriend, Brady Jones. Chloe had never had a boyfriend for the holidays before. *Maybe dating Brady could help Chloe fall back in love with Christmas?*

Chloe couldn't help grinning like an idiot as she let the promise of a new year fill her with hope. Thinking about her boyfriend made her giddy. With thoughts of kissing Brady making her feel she could float away, Chloe pushed through the double doors to find him. *This was going to be the best year ever.*

1

Chloe

DECEMBER 22ND

Dear Journal,
Tomorrow is the first day of winter break.
I can't wait to have ten days without seeing Brady.
This has been the worst year ever . . .

CHLOE LURKED OUTSIDE the red double doors of Westerly High. She gulped frigid winter air into her lungs as she peered around the icy parking lot to make sure she didn't see Brady's SUV. Icicles clung to the bare, frostbitten trees, sending a shiver racing up her spine with each gust of blustery wind.

The weather in upstate New York was unforgiving in

December. Chloe always hated this time of year and even though in just a few short hours she'd be able to escape the halls of her high school for winter break, she couldn't manage to feel hopeful. Not in a tiny town like Pine Island, where she was constantly surrounded by Christmas cheer and happy couples.

A frown hardened her face as she realized perhaps the only two things she had to look forward to this winter break were not seeing Brady and not having to tell her sister they'd broken up.

Margot was three years older than Chloe, but this year was the first the sisters had ever spent apart. Margot had gone to a community college for two years before transferring to a university in New York City.

Chloe missed her like crazy. Margot, Chloe and Brady had been inseparable growing up. And it had only been because of Margot's meddling that Chloe had even managed to get a date with Brady in the first place. They may have grown up together, but Chloe didn't run in the same social circles as her popular older sister or her gym class hero crush, Brady.

But by some miracle Margot's plan of Chloe bringing Brady lemonade while he was cutting the grass at their family tree farm over the summer had actually worked—*mostly because Margot kept making Chloe wear her bikini tops when she did so.*

Chloe was about six inches shorter than her gorgeous older sister. And though they shared the same hazel eyes and chestnut hair, Chloe always felt like the less pretty version of her glamorous sister. It didn't help that the six inches that Chloe lacked on Margot in height, she made up for elsewhere —*mostly in boobs and butt.*

Chloe always said if they were both dancers, Margot would be a ballerina and Chloe would be J-Lo. Of course Margot said she'd kill for Chloe's curves, but what did she know? She didn't have to try to shove those curves into all of Margot's model-sized hand-me-downs. But Chloe had done it, because Margot had said the magic words. *'Trust me.'* And that was one phrase the sisters didn't throw around lightly.

So every day last summer, Chloe squeezed herself into Margot's skimpy bikinis and tight jean shorts and hiked through the rows of Christmas trees to bring Brady an ice cold lemonade while he worked on her parents' farm. And despite how terribly uncomfortable Chloe felt putting herself out there, Brady must've seen something he liked because by the third week of lemonades and flirting he pulled her up onto the tractor and kissed her.

Chloe remembered it all perfectly. How Brady's lips tasted like cherry chapstick, how she could feel the warmth of his skin against hers for hours afterward and how she'd run back to the house to tell Margot all about it.

But that was all in the past now. Margot had gone away to college and shortly after, Chloe's summer romance with Brady had crumbled. It'd been three months since she caught her supposed perfect boyfriend making out with the head cheerleader, Maci Martin, but it still hurt like it had been only yesterday.

It didn't help that Chloe had to watch Brady and Maci making out in the halls of her high school every day since. They were the perfect couple—*the basketball star and the cheerleader*.

They made much more sense on paper than Chloe and Brady ever had. But even knowing that did little to soothe the pain of having her heart broken. Chloe always thought her first love would be something to look back on fondly, and maybe it could've been if she hadn't been made to feel like such an utter fool by being the one to catch Maci and Brady making out. Everyone had seen them. It was beyond humiliating.

All Chloe wanted to do was cry and call her sister to tell her everything. Margot always knew exactly what to do in a crisis.

But catching up with her wasn't as easy as walking across the hall anymore. Chloe had to catch her sister between classes or sorority parties. And by the time Chloe got Margot on the phone she didn't feel like dredging up the painful details of Brady's betrayal anymore. Plus, Margot had news of her own. She'd met a boy!

Chloe could hear the excitement in her sister's voice when she told her all about Owen Hall and their amazing first date in Manhattan, so when Margot asked about Brady, Chloe hadn't wanted to dampen her sister's spirits.

Chloe had stupidly said, "We're good."

That was the only lie Chloe could remember ever telling her sister. And though it had started out innocent at first, it had grown over the past few months into an unstoppable monster. Chloe couldn't believe she'd managed to keep the truth from Margot for this long, but somehow she knew telling her sister what happened would only make it hurt worse.

Chloe's parents knew she and Brady had broken up, but not the details of how and why. But Margot would want to know it all. Which is what prompted Chloe to keep avoiding the truth. But now, for about the millionth time since her sister left for college, Chloe found herself missing Margot.

Margot wasn't only her sister, but her best friend. Maybe telling Margot the awful truth about how Brady broke her heart would help Chloe find a way to heal. If anything Margot would certainly find a way to distract Chloe for a while. She always knew how to fix things. Like when Chloe's bike got stolen in fourth grade or when she didn't make the cheerleading team in fifth or when her favorite cat ran away in seventh. Margot always made Chloe a piping hot mug of hot cocoa and then spent hours in front of the fireplace with her concocting over-the-top s'more creations with everything they found in the pantry.

When they were done, Margot would say, "Feel better now, Co-Co?"

And she always did.

Chloe smiled at the memory. She didn't really know which had come first, her love of cocoa or her nickname, but either way both seemed to stick. Just like Margot's nickname of Go-Go, born out of Chloe's toddler talk.

Margot was pretty much the only one who still called Chloe, Co-Co. She hadn't realized how much she missed hearing her nickname until that moment. Chloe's eyes welled as it fully hit her that this would be the first Christmas she wouldn't get to spend with her big sister. Margot was going on a trip to Italy with her sorority over winter break. That meant, not only would Chloe not get any sister time this holiday, but she would also be picking up the slack at the family Christmas tree farm all on her own.

She grimaced at the thought as her boots squeaked down the hallway leaving little puddles of melted snow in her wake. *Maybe she would just sleep through winter break this year.*

Brady

Brady Jones flashed his all-star grin as he jogged past a group of gushing girls. He'd never get used to it—*being so popular*. Not that he wasn't before, but this year was a whole new level of awesome. Being the starting quarterback *and* captain of the basketball team had raised his hall cred tremendously.

Since basketball started two weeks ago it seemed like flirting was the new hazing in the hallways. The girls' pick up lines hit harder than his linemen.

"Are you gonna ask me out soon or do I need to call 'delay

of game'?" one of the girls called after him, sending the rest of her friends into a fit of giggles.

Brady just smiled. "You know I'm with Maci."

"For now," one called back.

"Yeah, you could always *Chloe* her," another called. "We won't tell."

Inside, Brady cringed, but he gave the girls a salute and continued down the hall. He still felt bad for the way Chloe found out about him and Maci. He hadn't planned to hurt her. *But when Maci Martin kisses you, it's not like you could say no.*

Speaking of Maci . . . Her gorgeous silhouette was leaning against Brady's locker waiting for him. "Hey, hot shot," she purred, stretching up on her toes to kiss him. "You ready for the ski trip?"

"You know it," he replied, sweeping her off her feet.

As she kissed him a group of guys walking by started to applaud. Brady smirked between kisses. *Senior year was so awesome.*

2

Ethan

"Come on, bro. It's my year to pick," Owen argued.

Ethan Hall growled at his brother as he continued stuffing board shorts and t-shirts into his duffle bag. "Yeah, but this wasn't really your choice, was it?"

"It'll be fun, E."

"For you maybe, but I don't really care about going to some cheesy Christmas wonderland to meet your girlfriend's parents."

"If you gave her a chance you might like her," Owen argued.

"Brother, I could give her a million chances and I'm still not going to like her. She's like an over-caffeinated Chihuahua."

Owen got that stupid giddy smile on his face that Ethan loathed. It was the same lovesick expression he always got when thinking about his girlfriend. "Yes, but she's *my* over-caffeinated Chihuahua and I want you to like her, E."

Ethan rolled his eyes. "She took Bermuda from me so she's not off to a good start."

"We've been to Bermuda the past three Christmases," Owen replied.

"And what's wrong with that?"

"Variety is the spice of life, little brother. You should try it sometime," Owen said with a peppy wink. "Besides, we can go to Bermuda next year."

"Damn straight we will. Next year I get to pick where we spend Christmas."

Owen laughed. "Fine. But this year, I'm in charge and I say we're going to the Everett's Christmas Lodge and Tree Farm. So if you don't want to freeze to death, you should probably pack something other than shorts and t-shirts."

Ethan shrugged. "We'll see."

"I'm not going to change my mind, bro. You need to get on board or you're not going to enjoy Christmas."

"When is Christmas ever enjoyable?"

Owen's face softened. "That's what I'm trying to change, Ethan. Maybe it's time you try, too." With that, he walked out of their dorm room.

Ethan sighed heavily. He hated when he pushed his brother too far. He didn't mean to. Owen was the only other person on the planet who understood why the holidays were so hard for Ethan. Usually, they were on the same page and commiserated together on some far away beach with sunshine and cocktails to help them forget why they hated Christmas, but everything was different this year.

Owen's new girlfriend had brought a happiness back to him that Ethan hadn't seen in years. Ethan should be happy for his brother, and for the most part he was, but not during the holidays. During the holidays, Ethan wanted his brother to himself so he had someone else to share his pain. He was the only family Ethan had left, so the fact that

Owen's girlfriend was stealing him was another strike against her.

"Maybe it's time I try?" Ethan muttered to himself. "How can he even say that?" Ethan grumbled as he continued to slam vacation attire into his duffle bag. "I try every single day."

And he did. But no amount of trying would make him forget he'd lost his mother on Christmas Eve all those years ago. Ethan knew his brother was in love and that was why he had a new, shiny attitude about the holidays, but Ethan didn't see the point of love. It didn't last. He'd loved his mother, but cancer didn't care about love or family or holidays. It took what it wanted, when it wanted. It didn't make exceptions for love. If it had, their mother would still be here because Ethan couldn't imagine another woman being loved more than he'd loved her.

He finished packing and sat down on his bed with a tired sigh. He hated how easy it seemed for everyone but him to move on. His father had moved on, remarrying and starting a new family, and now Owen was moving on with his energetic new girlfriend from the middle-of-nowhere New York.

Ethan rubbed his face and glanced at his reflection in the mirror. *What was wrong with him? Why couldn't he move on?*

He sighed again as he found himself wondering if maybe some people just weren't meant to find happiness.

Chloe

The late bell rang and Chloe looked up from her desk even though she told herself not to. She knew who would be striding through the door. He was always the last one to class because he spent all his time sucking Maci's face in the mistletoe-laden halls. And even though Chloe knew better than to glance at the door, she couldn't stop herself.

As she watched Brady walk in her heart plummeted. Today was one of the days he didn't even look at her and for some reason that hurt worse than the days he did. It was like she didn't even exist anymore and she couldn't understand that. They'd known each other since they were ten. And they'd spent the entire summer and the first few weeks of senior year *really* getting to know each other.

Brady had been her first everything. First kiss, first boyfriend, first love, first . . . Her cheeks flushed as she remembered all their other firsts. *God, she was so stupid. How had she ever thought he loved her?*

Mr. Tanner started droning on about their history papers and Chloe put her head down, squeezing her eyes shut tight as she willed her tears away. *Only a few more hours,* she told herself. *Then you can go home and have a break from boys and broken hearts.*

She was looking forward to ten days without having to see Brady and Maci in the halls. And for once she was glad her parents were making her miss the Westerly ski trip to work at the tree farm. All summer she'd been scheming how to get out of helping over the holidays to go on the ski trip with Brady, but her worrying had been premature. It was Maci going on the ski trip with Brady now.

Nothing had worked out the way Chloe had expected this year. The heaviness of that made her feel suddenly tired. So tired that she didn't bother reopening her eyes as she drifted off to the sound of Mr. Tanner's monotone voice.

Chloe was still having trouble getting her new locker combination to work. She spilled her pumpkin spice latte on her new corduroy skirt and took so long cleaning it in the bathroom that she was late meeting Brady at his locker.

Brady. Chloe gave an involuntary sigh just thinking about him—his big blue eyes, sandy brown hair and chin dimple. She picked up her pace knowing his pillow-soft lips were waiting for her. Her white converse squeaked down the red and white-checkered hallway as Chloe made her way to the bank of senior lockers. Her heart was already pounding with anticipation, but when she saw the back of Brady's football jersey, her heart sped to triple time. There was just something so indescribable about being his.

She'd liked him for so long but had always been too afraid to do anything about it for fear of Brady not liking her back. But he did like her. He'd chosen her this summer and it was exhilarating.

As she got closer, Chloe decided to tiptoe, thinking it would be funny to sneak up behind Brady and wrap her arms around him. His broad shoulders were angled toward his locker. Whatever he was staring at must've been enthralling because he had yet to notice her. But as Chloe got closer she suddenly found herself wishing she hadn't decided to sneak up on her boyfriend. Because all at once she realized exactly what Brady found so interesting. *Maci Martin!*

Her lips, to be more exact.

The head cheerleader was attached to Brady's face!

Heat started at Chloe's cheeks and raced down to her toes when she saw them. They hadn't seen her and she had plenty of time to back away, but she couldn't seem to tear her eyes away. She knew she should. This was embarrassing on so many levels but she couldn't move. She could barely breathe. *Wait, was she breathing?*

A sharp pain in her chest reminded her to take a breath. But she couldn't catch it. Panic began to set in as Chloe realized she needed to leave before she burst into the strangling sobs that were flooding her throat. But her hands were shaking so badly she couldn't hold onto her books. They clattered to the floor in the hallway and her favorite pen rolled across the floor until it hit Maci's shoe.

Maci pulled her face away from Brady's and looked at Chloe with her big brown doe eyes. "Oh," Maci said. "I'm sorry, do I have something that belongs to you?" she asked, pointing a perfectly manicured finger at Brady.

Chloe nodded her head and both Brady and Maci exploded into hysterical laughter. The hallway suddenly packed with students and all of them joined in the pointing and laughing. Struggling away from the crowd, Chloe darted down the hall, but at every turn Brady and Maci reappeared, until finally they were blocking her from the exit.

Brady's blue eyes sparkled as he looked at Chloe without an ounce of shame. "Chloe! Hey, I didn't see you there."

"Clearly!" she yelled.

Brady scratched the back of his head and gave her his easy grin. "So, this is awkward . . ."

"Are you two together?" Chloe asked.

Maci grinned. "It appears so."

"Since when?" Chloe squawked.

Maci giggled and Brady shrugged. "Now, I guess?"

Maci nodded, linking her fingers with his.

Chloe just blinked at them completely dumbfounded.

"Are you sure you're okay?" Maci asked. "Your face is super red."

"Yeah," Brady added. "You kinda have Margot's murdery look in your eyes."

Chloe schooled her features. "I'm perfectly fine," she lied.

"Well, in that case . . ." Brady turned back toward Maci and started kissing her like she was his only source of oxygen.

Chloe's dignity could only take so much. She pushed past them and ran into the parking lot, tears leaking down her cheeks—*because she most certainly wasn't fine.*

Buzz!

The bell rang and Chloe jumped in her seat. She looked around the classroom as students bustled by. Quickly, she felt her cheeks to see if the tears had been real. *They were dry.* It was only a dream.

Chloe collected her things and tried to pinch some life back into her cheeks as she made her way toward to door. Before she could escape, Mr. Tanner called out to her.

"Miss Price?"

"Yes?"

"Are you feeling well?"

"Yes."

"I couldn't help noticing you had your head down in class."

Chloe's cheeks burned. "I'm sorry, Mr. Tanner. I'm just tired. I've been busy with work after school."

He smiled warmly. "Ah, yes. The farm's open late hours until Christmas, isn't it?"

She nodded.

"Well, only a few more days, then you can get some rest. I don't want you sleeping in class, young lady."

"I'm sorry, Mr. Tanner. It won't happen again."

"If you have your father get me an invite to your famous Christmas Eve party, I think I can let it slide," he said with a wink.

"I'll ask him," Chloe said, taking the opportunity to escape.

She sighed with relief once in the hall. Most of the time she hated that her parents ran a Christmas tree farm. It meant Christmas was a business, which kinda took the magic out of the holiday for Chloe. But sometimes it came in handy.

The farm and newly added lodge were extremely popular and nearly fully booked during the winter months. But that didn't stop everyone in their small town of Pine Island from trying to leverage an in. But if it got Mr. Tanner off her back, Chloe was glad to work the system.

She hadn't been at her best these past few months and that nightmare she'd had in his class this morning had happened on more than a few occasions. Thankfully, Mr. Tanner's class was the only one Chloe had with Brady this semester. It frustrated her to no end that she still let Brady have such a hold on her. *How long was she going to let her mind relive the humiliating moment of getting dumped?*

Things hadn't happened exactly like the nightmare. Brady and Maci hadn't magically appeared in the hallway just to make out in front of her. And no one had pointed and laughed at her, but everyone *had* seen her reaction when she walked up to catch her boyfriend sucking Maci's face. It hadn't been fun. And neither was reliving nightmare versions of it.

Chloe had a queasy feeling in her stomach for the rest of her day as she did her best to avoid all the places she knew Brady and Maci might be hanging out. Unfortunately, Chloe's luck ran out after lunch when she barreled straight into Brady coming out of the bathroom.

Chloe felt his strong arms circle around her, the deep tenor of his voice vibrating through her as he gave her a teasing, "Whoa there, Clo."

"S-sorry," she stuttered, trying to back away from him so quickly she knocked into someone else in the busy hall.

Brady steadied her again and before she could get away he spoke. "So, how've you been?"

"What?" she replied, dumbfounded.

He stuffed his hands in his pockets and shrugged. "I haven't seen you around much."

Was he serious? Why the heck would he see her around? Even if he'd been looking it's not like he could see much past Maci's perfect lips, which was where he spent most of his time.

When she didn't respond, Brady spoke again, lowering his voice. "I just want to make sure you're okay."

Chloe gave a laugh. "You're worried I'm not okay?"

"Yeah, we're friends, right?"

"Friends? Are you kidding me, Brady?"

"Look Chloe, we've known each other forever. Can't we find a way not to be weird around each other?"

"When are we ever around each other, Brady?"

"I don't know. School, next door, the Christmas Eve party . . ."

Chloe frowned. "I know it must really suck that you have to see me at school and be my neighbor, but don't worry, in a few months we'll both graduate and go to college and we'll never have to see each other again. And as far as the Christmas Eve party, you'll be on a ski trip with Maci, so you can stop worrying about me being weird because you won't have to deal with it."

It was Brady's turn to frown. "Is that really what you want? To never see me again?"

"Why do you care?"

Brady

Why did he care?

He genuinely liked Chloe. She was one of his oldest friends and they'd had *a lot* of fun this summer. *But was that it? Were they just a convenient fling?* He couldn't help wondering if they could've been more if Maci hadn't intervened.

Before Brady could come up with an answer for Chloe he saw Maci walking down the hall toward him. The bright smile that had been plastered on her pretty face began to slide when she saw him talking to Chloe. *Crap!* She'd expressly told him she didn't like him hanging around Chloe.

Brady squeezed the back of his neck to release his stress. He could only handle one difficult conversation at a time and knowing Maci wasn't going to be happy about his latest news he decided to cut his conversation with Chloe short. But by the time Brady turned back to her, Chloe was already walking away.

He watched as Chloe hustled away from him, her boots squeaking noisily down the hall. *Dammit.* He honestly hadn't wanted to hurt her—*again.*

He'd set out to apologize and smooth things over before winter break. This thing with Maci wasn't premeditated. It just sort of happened.

They'd been flirting after football practice over the summer but he hadn't thought anything more would happen. It was just some innocent fun until Maci snuck up on Brady and covered his eyes at his locker that first week of school. He'd honestly thought it was Chloe that day until he'd felt Maci's tongue go down his throat. *Chloe didn't kiss like that. But hot damn was that a kiss.*

Still, Brady had known Chloe since they were kids. He hated that he'd treated her poorly. She deserved better and he wanted to make things right between them. His conscious told him it was the right thing to do, but the rest of him was telling his conscious to shut the hell up. He had Maci Martin on his arm. *Freaking Maci Martin!* Head cheerleader and most gorgeous girl at Westerly High. Brady would be an idiot to screw that up. *And thanks to his coach, he still might.*

"Hey," Maci said, her normally cheery voice guarded. "Were you just talking to your ex-girlfriend?"

"I was talking to my friend and neighbor," Brady corrected.

She narrowed her charcoaled eyes and cocked her head to the side in that way she did when she was aggravated. "About what?"

"Nothing. I was really waiting to talk to you."

Her smile returned. "Really? What do you want to talk to me about?"

"Winter break."

Maci bounced on her toes. "Yay! I'm soooo excited about spending it with you. The ski trip is going to be amazing! I booked a suite with a hot tub," she said coyly.

Brady bit his lip, mentally cursing his basketball coach for scheduling a tournament in the middle of what Brady was anticipating to be the best weekend of his life. "About the ski trip . . ." Brady started. "How mad would you be if I couldn't go?"

Maci's eyes narrowed again.

3

Ethan

ETHAN STARED out the window in disgust. The snow was so bright he had to wear his sunglasses. *At least something he'd packed for Bermuda had come in handy.* He couldn't believe he was actually crammed in the back of an old Toyota 4-Runner on a road trip to meet his brother's girlfriend's family.

Ethan wasn't the biggest fan of the bubbly girl, but since it was Owen's year to choose he didn't have much choice in the matter. The Hall boys had a lot of strange traditions—*some born from being brothers, others from their unfortunate childhood.* But at least they had each other. That was one thing that Ethan hoped would never change. Although Ethan had a sneaking suspicion if Owen's girlfriend had her way, Ethan wouldn't get any time with his brother. As it was they seemed to spend every waking hour together. It was beyond annoying. Especially since Ethan and Owen shared a tiny college apartment.

It was challenging at times; being so dependent on his brother. But after suffering the losses they had, Ethan was determined to keep the little family he had left. So that's how he found himself on the tail end of a road trip to upstate New York to spend Christmas with a family of strangers.

"It's every bit as pretty as you said, babe," Owen murmured from the driver's seat.

Unlike Ethan, Owen wasn't wearing sunglasses. Instead he was squinting like an idiot as he took in the quaint surroundings of the wintery rural town. It was a far cry from Manhattan.

"Hard to believe we're still in New York, " Ethan muttered.

Owen had just pulled off the exit into the little town of Pine Island. They'd passed dozens of billboards for Everett's Christmas Lodge and Tree Farm on the way, boasting they did Christmas better than the North Pole.

"Don't be a city kitty," Owen's girlfriend said, smirking at Ethan in the rearview mirror. "You'll love it here. It grows on you, I promise."

Ethan found himself rolling his eyes for the millionth time. He honestly didn't know what the hell Owen saw in Margot Price. In Ethan's opinion, she tried too hard. She was always so perfectly dressed, her hair and makeup flawless, her smile dialed up way too high, her enthusiasm even higher. It was exhausting being around her. It wasn't one thing in particular that Ethan didn't like. It was just the total sum of her overly happy parts.

He glared at Margot's endless smile in the rearview. She was easily the prettiest girl Ethan had ever disliked. Sighing, he found himself hoping this trip would go horribly wrong and Owen would finally break up with Margot. It would certainly be nice to have his brother back. For a second, the thought lifted Ethan's spirits, but as he watched Owen lean over and kiss Margot at every stoplight, his hopes evaporated.

Owen was way too smitten to even notice if Margot's family

was full of lunatics. Which Ethan was sure they were. In his opinion, anyone who celebrated Christmas every day and spawned a daughter that smiled as much as one of Santa's elves must have a few screws loose.

"We should be there in about forty-five minutes," Owen added.

"Great," Ethan replied, sarcastically. "I'm starving. Can we stop and pick something up for dinner?"

"No way," Margot replied. "My parents will want to cook us dinner."

Ethan mock strangled Margot for the third time this trip, but of course she didn't notice. She was too busy snapping a picture of herself and Owen at a stoplight. She'd been documenting the entire drive.

Laughing, Margot turned and snapped a photo of Ethan to add to her feed. "You're too funny, E. You've really perfected your Scrooge face. My family is just going to eat you up!"

Ethan let out an exasperated sigh and glared at his brother in the rearview. Owen smirked, knowing that Ethan hadn't really been joking when he pretended to wrap his hands around Margot's skinny neck.

"Can we bring anything to dinner?" Owen asked.

But Margot was so engrossed in posting her photos she didn't respond.

"Margot," Owen said more forcefully.

"Hmm?"

"I was asking you a question," Owen continued patiently.

"Oh, I'm sorry, baby. This photo of us is just the cutest. I made it my new background on my phone. See."

Owen grinned and kissed her. "You're the cutest."

"No, you are."

"I'm gonna be sick, " Ethan muttered.

Owen smiled and repeated his original question, while Ethan cracked his knuckles praying he'd never meet a girl who could turn him into the pathetic sap that Owen now was. *What the hell was the draw?* Ethan stared at Margot trying to see what his brother saw. *Maybe she was phenomenal in bed?*

Ethan snorted. *Of course she was. Everything was phenomenal in Margot's sparkly snow globe world.* Ethan shook his head, smirking at his own joke until his brother's words recaptured his attention.

"So they don't know we're coming?" Owen asked.

Margot grinned. "Nope! I thought it would be fun to surprise them. I can't wait to see their faces!"

A sinking feeling settled in Ethan's gut. This trip just kept getting worse and worse. Not only was he being dragged along on this holiday honeymoon, but he knew from experience that no one loved surprise guests.

Chloe

December 22nd

Dear Journal
One more class until this day is officially over. Thank God! All I want to do is drink hot cocoa and cuddle up in front of the fireplace with my dog. It's the only thing I'm looking forward to this Christmas. But I most likely won't even get to do that much. Mom and Dad are going to need me to work around the clock at the lodge. And since Margot isn't coming home I won't even manage to have any fun while I'm working. Is there any way to fast-forward to college?

Chloe stared down at her journal. She was in Mrs. Murphy's English class. No one was paying any attention to her. Christmas-itis had officially set in. And if Chloe was honest, she'd caught the fever, too. Running into Brady in the hall earlier had solidified her need to get over him. She couldn't live like this. She wanted to move on already . . . to find things to look forward to again.

Flipping back through the pages of her journal would reveal nothing but the musings of a broken-hearted girl. And Chloe didn't want to be that girl. The sappy one who couldn't get over the first guy she fell for. But no matter how hard she tried she couldn't seem to get Brady's rejection out of her head. It was maddening.

She didn't know what she was waiting for. It's not like Margot was going to come home and magically fix everything. Chloe needed to get used to figuring things out for herself. Maybe that's why being cast aside by Brady hurt so badly. It made Chloe realize she was truly on her own.

She rubbed her eyes with the heels of her hands until she saw spots. She just wanted today to end. It's not like she was looking forward to an exciting winter break, but at least she wouldn't have to sit around listening to everyone else talking about their amazing plans. *Bitter, party of one.*

All of Chloe's plans for the perfect senior year had deflated. Every time she saw Brady and Maci in the hall, pain seized her. But the thing that hurt even worse than getting dumped was that she'd lost her friend. Besides Margot, Brady had been one of Chloe's closest friends before he'd kissed her and catapulted himself out of the friend zone.

At the time, Chloe hadn't realized that meant they wouldn't be able to go back. Her stupid optimism had never let her imagine that things might not work out. Of course now she knew how ridiculous that was. It's not like many people found their soulmate in high school. *Actually, at ten years old if she wanted to be technical.*

Brady moved into the only other house on their street the

summer before fifth grade. For as long as Chloe could remember he'd been a fixture in her life and she'd never imagined it any other way. Maybe all of this was her fault for holding her feelings back.

She'd known she had a crush on him for a long time, but she'd been too afraid to tell him. Chloe blew out a breath in frustration, realizing she'd allowed her fear to have a hand in ruining her chances with Brady. If she'd told him how she felt earlier they would've had a stronger relationship and he wouldn't have been tempted by Maci.

Today had been the perfect opportunity to talk to Brady. She should've told him how upset she was and that she missed her friend. *Why hadn't she?*

Chloe let her forehead sink to the desk. *Too late now.*

There had to be something she could do to get over her misery. Maybe the long winter break would do it. She told herself she was grateful she wasn't going on the Westerly ski trip. She'd never gone. She always had to work. She tried to tell herself she didn't mind, that she preferred to observe the winter weather from the warmth and safety of her home. It wasn't really true, but sometimes if she told herself something enough, she started to believe it.

What Chloe really wanted to do was go ice skating with her family or build snowmen in the front yard or have snowball fights. They hadn't done any of those things since she was a little girl. It seemed every year the farm got busier and there was less and less time for fun. *It was strange how the family business seemed to be ruining her sense of family.*

Chloe tried to shake the sadness that thought evoked. Instead she focused on her hopes for curling up by the fire with a novel and a mug of cocoa. That was still a good time in Chloe's book.

She laughed to herself realizing how much Brady would

hate that idea. *Why was she so devastated over losing a boy who was completely wrong for her?*

Brady was athletic and adventurous. He hated sitting still. Working at the farm over the summer had exhausted Chloe but Brady loved it. When she had a rare moment to herself she'd wanted to lay in her hammock and cuddle with her boyfriend, but Brady always wanted to play volleyball or drag her to parties. She was quiet and didn't really like crowds. He was outgoing and craved attention. She liked reading medical books or cheesy romance novels. He liked watching gory movies where people were always getting blown apart. She wanted to be a nurse or maybe even a doctor. He wanted to be a hunting guide like his father. She was a vegetarian. He ate meat like a boxer trying to make weight. She loved classical piano music. He loved old school rap. The list went on and on.

At first, Chloe thought their differences kept things interesting, but in the end they'd never been on the same page because they didn't have much in common. Of course Brady had chosen Maci. They made sense—*the jock and the cheerleader, not the nerd.*

Chloe picked her head up and forced herself to stop wallowing in self-pity. Just because things hadn't worked out with Brady didn't mean she'd never find love. Chloe was a glass half-full kind of girl or at least she wanted to be. She couldn't help it. Growing up in a family that celebrated Christmas year-round bred joy into the soul. She didn't want to let one failed relationship ruin her.

Enough was enough. She was going to give herself winter break to get over Brady for good. She'd just lock away that part of her heart, bury herself in college research and then she would return to school refreshed and with a new attitude. No more excuses. A boy cleanse was all she needed . . .

4

Chloe

CHLOE WALTZED into the year-round Christmas wonderland that was her home, dropped her backpack by the door and stomped the snow off her boots. "Mom, I'm home," she called over the blaring holiday music.

It was some pop star making a mockery of a perfectly good Christmas classic and of course her mother was belting the tune right along with the singer. She didn't hear Chloe over the racket, but Chloe didn't mind. She was already occupied by Darcy whose little tail was zipping back and forth so quickly it was a tawny blur.

"How are you, my favorite little man?" Chloe asked scooping the dog up.

Darcy gave her a million sloppy kisses on her face. Chloe snuggled the dog close to her chest. She and Darcy shared a special bond and he always had a way of making her feel better.

Darcy looked dashing in today's outfit—a red cable-knit sweater with white snowflakes. Chloe couldn't help but smile when she saw him in it. The tiny dog probably had more clothes than she did, but that was because everyone in the family spoiled him rotten.

The little Yorkie had captured her heart three years ago. It had been love at first sight for Chloe when she saw him at the pet adoption drive at her local grocery store. She'd filled out the paperwork and taken him home that day. It was the one and only time she'd ever done something so bold without asking her parents' permission. But luckily, Darcy had easily won them over. *Who wouldn't melt when a five-pound ball of love licked them?*

Chloe grinned as she carried her dog into the kitchen, letting Darcy's excitement lift her spirits.

"Hey, sweetie!" her mother called. "I didn't hear you come in."

"I can't imagine why," she teased, referring to the blaring music.

Her mother turned it down. "How was school?"

Chloe shrugged. "It was school."

"Are you excited for winter break?"

"Absolutely!"

Her mother looked startled. "That's the most enthusiasm I've seen from you since—"

"Since he who shall not be named," Chloe interrupted.

She'd made a strict no-Brady-conversation rule since the day he dumped her and her mother wasn't very good at adhering to it.

"Right," her mother said pretending to zip her lips. "Well I'm glad you're home. Your dad could really use your help at the lodge. We booked a last minute wedding reception and now all the rooms are sold out. Do you think you can help at the front desk?"

Chloe groaned as she realized her plans for a quiet fireside evening were out. “Sure. Let me go get changed first.”

She padded up to her bedroom on the second floor and quickly changed out of her jeans and cardigan, swapping them for her khaki skirt and ugly Christmas sweater that the lodge staff all wore. Grumbling, she pulled on a pair of argyle socks and grabbed the Santa hat that completed the outfit.

Chloe looked longingly at her favorite pair of pink fuzzy pajama pants that hung on the back of her desk chair. Underneath, rested her favorite slippers of all time. Her parents got them for her for her birthday a few years back because they looked like mugs of hot cocoa. And as if that didn’t already make them the best slippers ever, they were heated! In the winter, toasty toes were a luxury. *Apparently a luxury that would have to wait until she was done with work.*

Washing her face and pulling her long dark hair into a messy braid, she tugged on the Santa hat and headed back downstairs with Darcy trotting merrily behind her. Halfway there her cellphone rang.

“Hello?”

Margot’s excited voice rang out on the other end. “Co-Co!”

“Go-Go?”

“Where are you?” Margot asked.

“Home. How’s Italy? Is it amazing? I want to hear all about it.”

Margot giggled. “I wouldn't know.”

Chloe frowned. “What do you mean? Mom said you arrived in Florence this morning.”

“Change of plans,” Margot said excitedly. “I'm coming home for Christmas!”

Chloe's heart stopped, her voice raising a whole octave. “Are you serious?”

“Of course I'm serious. I couldn't spend Christmas away from my favorite sister.”

"Oh my God, Margot you have no idea how excited I am to hear you're coming home."

"And it's not just me," Margot added. "I've got a surprise for everyone."

"A surprise?"

"Owen and his brother are coming with me!"

Disappointment filled Chloe's chest. For a brief second she thought she'd have her sister all to herself again, but those hopes were dashed the moment she said her boyfriend was coming with her. And apparently his brother. "Do Mom and Dad know?"

"No, I wanted it to be surprise."

They'll be surprised alright, Chloe thought. "Mom just told me the lodge is fully booked. Where are they going to stay?"

Their house was tiny. They didn't even have a guest room.

"Oh! I guess I hadn't thought of that," Margot replied. "Oh well, we'll figure it out. Maybe I can crash in your room like we used to when you had bunk beds and the boys can take my room."

Chloe's heart swelled. Memories of late night talks with Margot filled her with hope. "I'd love that."

"Good. Make sure everyone's home by dinner. I can't wait to see Mom and Dad's faces when I surprise them."

Chloe laughed. "Me too."

"See you soon, sis."

WITH THE ANTICIPATION of Margot's arrival, work flew by. Chloe had trouble dragging her father out of the office on time without telling him the reason he needed to be home. Luckily, the promise of fresh-baked Christmas cookies that she'd seen her mother starting when she'd left had done the trick.

Chloe had just enough time to take off her boots, Santa hat and pull her hair into a messy topknot when she heard a car pull into the driveway. Chloe's excitement soared as she raced to catch Darcy before the doorbell rang. Unfortunately, she wasn't fast enough. The *Jingle Bells* door chime started at the same time the oven timer went off in the kitchen. Darcy hated both and flew into a tizzy, unsure how to attack the door and oven simultaneously.

"Can you get the door?" Chloe's mother shouted from the kitchen.

"Trying. Gotta grab the gremlin first."

Chloe chased after Darcy, knowing opening the door without having him in hand wasn't an option. The dog might be little but he could run like a greyhound and Chloe had no desire to go racing through the snow. He was like Houdini when it came to getting through a door and as usual, Margot was ringing the doorbell a million times, making catching Darcy that much more difficult.

Finally, Chloe captured him. Wrenching open the door breathlessly, she was met with her sister's smiling face.

"Surprise!" Margot shrieked in an ear-piercing shout. She took a step into the house and gave Darcy a kiss before pulling Chloe into a warm embrace.

Darcy wriggled between them, annoyed at being smothered, but Chloe didn't care. Her sister was home. She could've cried right then, but their hug was cut short by the squeal of her mother. Both of Chloe's parents came rushing from the kitchen.

"Margot?" her father bellowed.

Her mother gasped. "Oh my God! I thought I heard my baby's voice! What are you doing here?"

"Surprise," Margot said again, dashing into their mother's arms.

Chloe was so excited by Margot's appearance that she'd

forgotten she wasn't alone until a male voice startled her. "Hi, I'm Owen, the boyfriend."

Chloe stared up into the handsome face of a stranger with jet-black hair and bright green eyes. He extended his hand and she shook it. "I'm Chloe, the sister."

"Wow! You two are almost identical. It's so nice to finally meet you," Owen said, enthusiastically before he followed Margot into the house to continue the introductions.

Chloe tried not to let her eyes follow Owen too closely, but he was one of the most beautiful people she'd ever seen in real life. He was wearing dress pants, a deep green collared sweater over a navy plaid shirt, and his watch looked like it cost more than Chloe's car. She briefly wondered if all boys in New York City looked like they'd just come from a cologne ad or if Margot had just won the boyfriend lottery? But then another male voice made Chloe jump.

A nearly identical tall, dark and handsome boy stood in the doorway. Chloe pressed her hand to her chest wondering if the stress of the past few months had finally caught up with her. *Was she having a stroke? How else could she explain seeing double?*

The boy gave her that crooked, cute boy smile that made it hard to breathe. *She was wrong. This* boy was the most beautiful person she'd ever seen. At first glance he seemed identical to Owen, but upon closer inspection there were many subtle differences. They both had the same impeccable fashion sense, dark hair and piercing green eyes, but the second boy had a quiet sharpness to him that made him breathtaking. Chloe couldn't look away.

"Don't worry, I'm used to the double take," he said. "We're not twins, but we get that a lot. I'm Ethan, the brother."

Chloe laughed nervously. "Oh. Okay. Thanks for clearing that up. I was starting to think I'd gone completely crazy."

Ethan's eyes tracked over Chloe's eclectic Christmas outfit, all the way down to her red and green argyle knee socks. *Clearly her wardrobe was putting her further into the crazy category.*

Ugh. Why hadn't she changed out of her uniform?

Ethan

Ethan had to look away from Chloe's face to stop the strange mix of emotions that were flooding him. When he'd first caught a glimpse of her something in his chest tightened. She was stunning in a torn down kind of way that surprisingly appealed to him. She wore no makeup and her hair looked like a chestnut tornado atop her head. Silky wisps floated around her rosy cheeks, framing her stunned face. As he took in the rest of her appearance, he only found himself more intrigued. She dressed nothing like Margot.

Ethan liked what Chloe's kitchy holiday outfit said about her. *Hear I am, take it or leave it.*

After the grueling car ride watching Margot do nothing but repeatedly snap selfies that she edited until she resembled a brunette Barbie, Chloe's rawness was refreshing. But then Owen ruined it by blurting out how much they resembled each other.

It was true. They both had the same dark chestnut hair, creamy pale skin, heart-shaped face, button nose and bright hazel eyes. But there was a soothing, calmness coming from Chloe that Margot was missing.

Though once Owen mentioned it, it was hard for Ethan to ignore how much Chloe looked like Margot. The instant desire to ball his hands into fists took over Ethan's mind, killing the initial spark he'd felt in his chest. But then he heard Chloe speak and it started again. Her voice wasn't anything like Margot's. It was soft and sweet, immediately making him think of marshmallows or some other delicious sugary treat he'd like to taste.

Get your mind out of the gutter, Ethan. This girl is in high school.

He gathered his thoughts and hauled their luggage into the house.

"Do you need help?" Chloe asked, making him like her even more.

His eyebrows pulled together in surprise. "Are you sure Margot's your sister?"

She gave a knowing laugh. "She gets forgetful when she's excited," Chloe said, grabbing one of Margot's many bags. "But yep, I'm her younger sister."

He frowned at that. "How much younger are we talking?"

"Three years," Chloe replied.

Ethan did a quick calculation. *That meant he was only a few months older than Chloe.*

Interesting . . .

Ethan fought against the hopefulness that climbed into his chest. He shook his head, realizing he was staring again. The girl was going to think he was some kind of freak. "I'm sorry. I just wasn't expecting you to be so different from your sister."

Chloe laughed. "Yeah, me too." Then she shrugged. "But I'm okay with it."

"Okay with what?"

"I'm the nerdy one and she's the pretty one."

Ethan felt his jaw muscles tick. "I think you need to get your eyes checked."

Chloe

CHLOE STOOD at the door in awe as she watched Ethan pick up the luggage and breeze past her. *'I think you'd better get your eyes checked?'* Maybe she needed to get her ears checked because it sounded like he was hitting on her.

No. Ethan's extreme gorgeousness must've melted Chloe's brain, because there was no way a boy who looked like that would ever find her attractive. Especially in her crazy Christmas outfit. She cursed her parents for being such Christmas nuts. *Why couldn't they just use normal uniforms like every other hotel in the world?*

Chloe sighed and shook her worries away, reminding herself that she was done with boys. This winter break was about finding herself.

basketball team, but he wasn't the star. That title belonged to Cooper Hanes.

So Brady wasn't surprised when he saw Maci waiting by Cooper's car after practice today. But that didn't stop Brady from feeling like shit.

Things had been purely physical between Brady and Maci —*which he wasn't complaining about.* He was an eighteen-year old boy. *That pretty much made him a walking erection.* But Brady found himself confused by the sudden emotional loss he felt. *Had he loved Maci?*

He'd loved the attention and the hooking-up, but they didn't have a friendship. Not like he and Chloe did. *Or used to.* Not counting today, Chloe hadn't spoken to Brady since they broke up.

Thinking of Chloe filled him with regret. Brady looked across his snow-covered lawn toward her house. Chloe's was the only other house on Pine Drive. She lived about three hundred yards away in an old log cabin that had been passed down from her great-great-grandfather, who started Everett's Christmas Tree Farm. Brady knew that because his mother was good friends with Chloe's mother.

The Price family had taken Brady's family under their wing when they moved to upstate New York. Brady had spent every summer and holiday playing with Chloe and Margot, and when he got older he spent them working at the tree farm. He had a lot of fond memories there. Regret seized him as he realized his poor decisions had cost him any future memories. *Or had they?*

He wondered if Chloe would give him another chance. *Christmas was the season of forgiveness, wasn't it?*

Brady looked harder at Chloe's little log cabin. There was a familiar SUV in her driveway and a ton of commotion on the front porch. Brady paused at his own porch to watch. Two dark-haired boys stood outside carrying luggage, while . . . *that shriek!*

Brady shivered. He'd know that shrill voice anywhere. *Margot was home.*

Chloe

Chloe sat at the dinner table stabbing at her salad. She couldn't believe Margot was home. She was practically bursting at the seams to pull her sister aside and ask her everything. She wanted to know all about college in New York City and her dreamy boyfriend, but most of all, she wanted to tell her sister what happened with Brady.

Chloe had said she was done with Brady, planning to put their issues aside and forget all about him during her winter break boy cleanse. But that was before she knew Margot was coming home for the holidays. There was no way she could spend the holiday in the same room with her sister without telling her what happened with Brady. Margot would surely ask about him.

Anxiety knotted Chloe's stomach as she realized she'd have to admit to her sister that she'd been lying to her for nearly three months.

"So how long are you all staying?" Chloe's mother asked excitedly.

Chloe watched Owen glance in his brother's direction. Their eyes met and Ethan's partial frown deepened. Owen's smile faltered only for a moment before he replied to Chloe's mother. "I'm not sure yet. We don't want to be an inconvenience."

"Nonsense," Chloe's mother said. "We're happy to have you. And Margot, I can't tell you how happy we are that you're here. The whole family is back together. It's a Christmas miracle."

Chloe glanced around the table of leftover pizza and salad.

It certainly didn't look like a miracle. But since Margot hadn't given much warning to her arrival, dinner was an improvised affair. Everyone was finished eating but Chloe's mother just kept gushing about how happy she was to have both her girls home for the holidays.

Her father was just as bad, reminiscing about meager holidays gone by when they didn't have enough money for gifts so they used to make them. That's how the ugly Christmas sweaters that were now the staff uniforms came about. Chloe's mother had made them.

The stories should've been embarrassing but Owen was all smiles as her father regaled them with story after story. It was obvious from the way the Hall Brothers dressed and their impeccable table manners that they came from money. Chloe could only imagine what they thought of her crazy Christmas cabin. Their home used to belong to her great-great-grandfather and was well over a hundred years old. Her great-great-grandfather, Everett, had built the place with his own hands—something that everyone in the family was proud of. But to two boys who'd come from New York City this place probably looked like a hunting shack full of Christmas crazy.

Chloe noticed the slight worry in her sister's eyes as if she were thinking the same thing. Chloe wanted to pull Margot aside and ask her what she'd been thinking bringing city boys out to the country. Obviously she'd promised them a beautiful Christmas at the lodge, not having the foresight to book a room. But that was Margot. She lived in the moment.

So far, Owen didn't seem deterred by the simple surroundings of the Price's home at all, but Ethan had a constant scowl on his face as his eyes roamed over the Christmas décor that cluttered the house year-round.

The other strange part of this whole evening was the way the two handsome strangers at the dinner table made Chloe feel. *Okay, it was really just Ethan.* When he wasn't looking around the small cabin with his judgy green eyes he was staring at Chloe. No one else seemed to notice, but Chloe couldn't help feeling nervous. She'd never been as outgoing as the rest of her family and the idea of spending a relaxing winter break with two guys, who could easily give David Beckham a run for his money, wandering the house seemed impossible. *How was Chloe supposed to relax in her ratty pajamas with them around?*

"So," Chloe's father was saying. "Where are you boys from again?"

"Manhattan, sir," Owen replied.

"Sir. I like that," Chloe's mother said, charmed by Owen's formalness. "So what brings you boys up here for the holidays?"

"Your daughter, ma'am," Owen replied, lacing his fingers through Margot's. "I'm just crazy about her. And when she mentioned spending Christmas together it was an offer too good to refuse."

Chloe's mother put down her fork. "I have to say, Margot, you two must be pretty serious to give up a trip to Italy."

Margot and Owen shared a conspiratorial look only people in love could manage. "We are," Margot replied.

Chloe's mother sighed. "Don't you just love, love?"

"We're happy to have you," her father said.

"That's right, the more the merrier I always say," her mother added.

Chloe caught Ethan staring at her again. Desperate for conversation to break his penetrating gaze that she asked, "Won't your family miss you this Christmas?"

Ethan and Owen exchanged another uncomfortable glance. Chloe swore Owen shook his head ever so slightly but Ethan answered anyway. "I doubt it since we weren't invited to spend Christmas with them."

A heavy silence settled over the dinner table making Chloe feel about two inches tall. *Why the hell had she asked that? Ugh.*

5

Brady

Brady limped up his driveway after basketball practice. He was ready for a long winter break to lick his wounds. Not only had he gotten his ass handed to him at practice today, but Maci broke up with him.

Talk about kicking a guy when he's down.

He shouldn't have been surprised. It was probably karma for the way things had ended with Chloe. Honestly, breaking up with her had been a mistake. Not only had he lost a girl he actually connected with, but a good friend, too. The way Maci dumped Brady when he told her that he couldn't go on the ski trip had him second-guessing everything.

It had been clear from the beginning that Maci was mainly interested in dating him because he was the high school hero of the moment. Once football season ended, things started to go downhill in their relationship. Brady was still captain of the

This was precisely why she preferred not to speak. She somehow always managed to put her foot in her mouth.

Finally, Owen cleared his throat. “Yeah, our family’s not big on the holidays. But we sure do appreciate you taking us in on such short notice like this.”

“Of course, sweetheart,” Chloe’s mother said. “Can I get anyone another slice of pizza?”

“No ma’am,” the boys replied in unison.

“Well, then how about we move to the living room for some Christmas cookies and eggnog?”

Everyone jumped at the opportunity to escape the awkwardness at the table. *And this time, Chloe felt she deserved the glare Ethan sent her way.*

6

Ethan

After Mrs. Price got them settled into Margot's tiny bedroom upstairs, Ethan started to dig through his duffle bag for some clean clothes. After a full day on the road and a bit of a tense dinner all he wanted to do was take a hot shower and get some sleep. If he could manage any at all in such a tiny bed.

So far Ethan wasn't sure following Owen to this cozy family Christmas was such a good idea. *Add that to the list of other dumb places I've followed him,* Ethan thought to himself.

Owen had promised they'd be staying in a five-star resort modeled to look like an old ski lodge. But somehow Ethan found himself sleeping in a tiny trundle bed next to his brother, in Margot's childhood bedroom. Not a good start.

Ethan sighed, realizing he'd rather be just about anywhere than here. But this was what happened when he let his brother make all his choices for him. Ethan's most recent poor choice was college. There was nothing wrong with Columbia University, except for the fact that it was only a few blocks from where they'd grown up in Manhattan.

Ethan had wanted a change of scenery after high school. He would have preferred to go somewhere new and exciting, like California or Europe. Somewhere where no one knew his name or the family history that came with it. But for the millionth time in his life, Ethan had put his own dreams on hold to keep his family intact. Just like he'd done on this trip.

For a split second he thought he might've found some silver lining in the random holiday vacation. Margot's sister had surprisingly caught Ethan's interest. But it was clear from the dinner conversation that he'd ruined any chances he had with her. Chloe didn't want them here.

It's just as well, he told himself. It's not like it could go anywhere with Chloe. Plus, it's not like Ethan really wanted to start something with his brother's girlfriend's nearly identical sister. Ethan huffed a laugh. *Yeah, that's not a recipe for disaster.*

"I'm gonna take a shower," Ethan muttered and headed out of the room.

Chloe

FINALLY, Chloe had a moment alone with Margot. The boys were getting settled into Margot's bedroom while Chloe busied herself pulling out her trundle bed to share with her sister for the rest of winter break.

"I can't believe the lodge is sold out," Margot mused while spreading a red and black buffalo check comforter out on the twin mattress. "Business must have really picked up."

Chloe nodded. "Ever since Mom and Dad started doing

weddings at the lodge the place has been booked solid. I wish you had called. Mom said we booked the last rooms today."

"Me too." Margot grimaced. "I really want the boys to have a good Christmas here."

Chloe bit her lip. "Yeah, it seems like Christmas is a sore subject, huh?"

Margot deflated. "Owen and Ethan lost their mother a few years back. It happened during the holidays and they don't have a relationship with their father so I know this is always a hard time for them."

"That's why you gave up Italy?" Chloe asked.

Margot looked nervously at her feet. "Mostly."

Chloe analyzed her sister's cryptic response. They never hid things from each other. "Mostly?"

Margot chewed her lip as she nodded. "I'm really falling for him, Co-Co. I think Owen might be the one. And I just couldn't bear the thought of him and his brother being alone on Christmas while I was in Italy. There was no way I could enjoy myself knowing what he was going through."

Chloe smiled. That was such a Margot thing to do. It was one of the things Chloe loved most about her sister—she always looked out for others. That's why this year had been so difficult without her. Chloe couldn't help thinking if Margot had been here things with Brady wouldn't have fallen apart the way they did.

Speaking of Brady, now was the perfect time to tell Margot the truth. Chloe took a deep breath, readying herself to relive her heartache all over again. But before she could get the words out something caught Margot's eye.

"Oh my God, Chloe! You kept this?"

Chloe's eyes met the embarrassing artwork hung at the bottom of her dry erase calendar. It was something she'd made for Margot a million years ago. It was a construction paper

Christmas tree with ornaments on it made from photographs of the two of them. “I really missed you, Go-Go.”

Margot sat down on the bed next to Chloe and hugged her tight. “I missed you, too, Co-Co.”

Chloe felt her eyes mist at the familiar comfort of being in her sister’s arms.

Margot pulled back to look at her. “Is everything okay?”

“Yeah. It’s just been lonely without you around.”

“I haven’t been gone that long.”

“Four months and six days,” Chloe added with a sniffle.

Margot’s mouth fell open. “You were counting?”

Chloe shrugged.

“Chloe, I know I’ve been busy with school, but you know I always have time for you, right?”

Chloe nodded. She needed to stop dragging her feet and rip the Brady-sized Band-Aid off already, but again they were interrupted. This time, by a knock on the door.

“Come in,” Margot called.

Owen peeked his head inside. “Hey, gorgeous.”

“Hey, yourself,” Margot greeted, leaping up off the bed to throw her arms around Owen’s neck.

“You didn't think I forgot about that winter wonderland walk you promised, did you?”

Margot giggled. “Never.”

Owen peeked around Margot's swinging brown ponytail to look at Chloe. “Your sister promised me a tour of the farm and lodge. Do you mind if I steal her?”

He was grinning like a kid at Christmas and it made it hard for Chloe not to like him, even though he was stealing her much-needed sister time. “No, it’s okay.”

“You sure?” Margot asked.

Chloe nodded.

Margot turned back to her boyfriend. “So are you sure you

can handle this, city boy? Everett's Christmas Tree Farm is pretty magical."

"So I hear," Owen replied, his smile growing.

"Is that what you're wearing?" Margot asked.

Owen was still dressed in his pressed pants, sweater and dress shirt. His dark eyebrows knitted together. "Is there a dress code?"

Margot laughed. "For the lodge? No. But there is one if you don't want to get frostbite on the walk there. Come on, silly. Let's go see if my dad has anything warmer you can borrow."

Margot started to push Owen from the bedroom but he turned around and said to Chloe, "I promise I won't keep her too long. I'm sure you two have a lot to catch up on. She talks about you *all* the time, you know?"

"I do not," Margot argued lightheartedly.

"Do too," he replied.

Margot playfully shoved Owen out of the bedroom, throwing Chloe a wink over her shoulder.

Their laughter trailed down the hallway making Chloe's heart sink. She remembered being that giddy about Brady not too long ago. *She hated how quickly things changed.*

7

Chloe

CHLOE HAD SHOWERED and washed up for bed and Margot still hadn't returned from her wintery walk with Owen. Not that Chloe could blame her sister. She remembered the feeling of being smitten all too well. If it had been Brady asking Chloe to take a walk through the winter wonderland of Christmas lights on the farm she would've spent all night out there not caring one bit if she couldn't feel her fingers and toes afterwards.

Brady's kisses had always been enough to keep her warm.

Despite her best efforts, tears trickled down Chloe's cheek as she thought of him. Wrong for her or not, she couldn't help missing him.

How was it that her house was bursting at the seams yet she still somehow felt alone?

There will be time to talk to Margot tomorrow, Chloe promised herself. And then she shut her eyes and welcomed sleep.

. . .

Ethan

It was nearly midnight when Ethan was awoken by his brother sneaking back into the bedroom. If he thought he was being quiet, it was a joke.

"You'd make a terrible spy," Ethan muttered as he listened to Owen climb into the creaky trundle bed next to his.

"Oh shut up, Watson."

Ethan smirked despite his bad mood. "You know, I don't remember ever agreeing that you got to be Sherlock."

Owen laughed. "I'm always Sherlock."

"And why's that?"

"Because I'm the charming, handsome one."

Ethan popped up on his elbow. "What does that make me?"

"The brooding, intelligent one, my dear Watson," Owen replied in a terrible British accent.

Ethan flopped back down onto the uncomfortable bed. "I'm going to get you back for this, you know?"

"For what? Inviting you to a nice Christmas where we can feel what it's like to be part of a normal family for a change?"

"They're not family," Ethan muttered.

"Not yet."

Ethan sat up again. "What does that mean?"

Owen ran a hand through his hair and sighed. "Nothing. It's just . . . would it kill you to try and enjoy a little holiday spirit?"

"Maybe I don't want to enjoy anything," Ethan said quietly, surprised at the truth in his words.

"Maybe that's your problem, E," Owen said gently. "You've gotta stop grieving and let yourself find some happiness, otherwise life's not worth living."

"Yes, screwing your grief away is a much healthier option."

Owen's hands hauled Ethan out of bed so quickly he yelped. "Watch what you say about my girlfriend, brother."

Ethan shook free of Owen's grasp. "Jesus, Owen. It was a joke." *Though really it wasn't.* Owen had a habit of losing himself in women whenever he needed a distraction. And since their mother died, there had been a long line of distractions. But Margot was the only one who'd ever stuck around this long, or been brave enough to invite him home.

"Well, I'm not joking," Owen growled. "Margot's the best thing that's ever happened to me, so don't screw this up, okay. I'm in love with her."

"That's what you said about the last one," Ethan muttered, startled by the ferocity in his tone.

"This time is different," Owen replied, his voice firm.

"Sure," Ethan replied.

"I'm serious, E. I want to make a good impression on Margot's family, so no more saying awkward shit that makes everyone uncomfortable."

"Oh, you mean you want me to lie to them? That's always a great way to make an impression."

"You don't have to lie, but you don't have to lay everything out in the open either."

"Are you referring to dinner?" Ethan asked.

"You know I am."

"You know where I stand on that," Ethan replied, defending his comment about not being invited to their family Christmas. Ethan didn't believe in sugar-coating things. He was unfortunately like his father in that respect. "If Margot and her family can't handle the truth then maybe you shouldn't be with her."

"No wonder you're single, E. You might as well wear a sign around your neck that screams, '*bitter and damaged, with a side of mommy issues*'."

Ethan stood up so swiftly he barely had time to control his clenched fists. He had an urge to punch something and if he didn't get out of this tiny bedroom soon, that something was going to be Owen's face.

He stomped to the hall and slammed the door behind him.

Chloe

It was just after midnight when Chloe awoke to a loud bang. She'd been sleeping soundly, but she had no idea how with the decibel of Margot's snoring. *Ugh. How had she forgotten that Margot snored like a lumberjack?*

This was going to be a rough ten days.

Chloe gave it her best effort, but she eventually gave up hope of falling back to sleep. Staring at the ceiling was doing her no good. Even counting her glow-in-the-dark stars couldn't help her mind from wandering back to her insensitive comment at the dinner table. *Why the hell had she asked about Owen and Ethan's family?* She wasn't trying to be rude. She just couldn't take the heat of Ethan's smoldering gaze. It was like looking into the eyes of a ghost—*beautiful and haunting.*

But worse than the guilt Chloe felt for putting the boys on the spot about crashing Christmas was the wounded look she'd seen in their eyes. *What kind of family didn't invite their own children to spend the holidays with them?*

Chloe knew better than to ask. Putting her foot in her mouth once was enough for one holiday. She wanted to let it go, but the longer she lay in bed the more she wondered what their story was. It was like she'd read the first chapter of an enticing mystery novel and then someone had snatched it away. Her inquisitive mind couldn't let it go. And the ideas her overactive imagination cooked up weren't going to let her get to sleep any time soon.

What if her sister had brought home serial killers that only murdered during Christmas? Far fetched, but plausible . . . *Why else would they not be invited to their own family Christmas?*

Chloe groaned and climbed out of bed. She decided to give up on sleep. Her mind was much too alert. Reading ahead on her course work for the fall would be a much better use of her time. She'd gotten into Columbia's nursing program and could use as much time as she could get to prepare for the intensive major. Anticipation filled her chest as she realized this would be the perfect time to take advantage of the quiet house and get some work done. She could curl up in front of the fireplace with some hot cocoa right now and start her prerequisite reading. *God knew she wouldn't have a chance to do it tomorrow now that Margot was home.*

With her heart set on a warm mug of heavenly chocolate, Chloe pulled on her bathrobe, stepped into her slippers, grabbed a laptop, her glasses and scooped Darcy off the bed. The little dog groaned in protest when she placed him on his feet. "Come on, boy. I'll give you another treat."

Darcy's ears perked up at the sound of his favorite word and he raced out of the room ahead of Chloe. It sounded like he was taking the stairs two at a time. Chloe grinned, shaking her head as she walked into the hall. She'd never known a dog so obsessed with treats. *Although, Chloe felt the same way about hot cocoa so she couldn't really blame him.* She had about a dozen different flavors in the pantry.

Distracted by thoughts of which cocoa to try first she didn't see the shadow coming from the bathroom until it was too late. Chloe smacked into a hard, cold chest and stumbled backwards. She would've fallen on her ass if a pair of solid arms hadn't wrapped around her like a pair of vice grips.

A tiny yelp escaped Chloe as she was crushed to an impeccably sculpted chest. She couldn't help noticing his anatomical perfection. Nor could she help breathing in the intoxicating college boy smell that clung to his skin. And the feel of his heart as it pounded against her cheek was impressive enough to stop time.

When Chloe caught her breath the world unfroze again. She stumbled away from the cocoon of warmth she'd been wrapped in. Disappointment seized her when she looked into the startled green eyes of Ethan, or was it Owen? It was hard to tell with her glasses mashed into her face. *Oh God, don't let it be Owen.*

She did *not* need to be having these feelings about her sister's boyfriend. Chloe had enough boy trouble as it was. "Sorry," she mumbled, backing away.

"Are you alright?" he asked, cautiously.

Definitely Ethan. His steely tone made her sure of it. "Fine," she muttered fixing her glasses.

"Do you always wear glasses?" he asked.

What a strange question. "Only when I read."

Ethan gave her a crooked grin. "I like them."

Chloe frowned. "Ethan, right?"

He nodded and the knot in Chloe's stomach eased.

"Good, because if you were Owen I was going to have a talk with my sister about dating guys who flirt with her little sister."

His dark eyebrows knitted together. "You're not that little, and who says I'm flirting?"

Chloe's cheeks instantly flamed. "No one—I mean—I thought . . ." *Stop talking, Chloe!* But for some reason she couldn't. It was like his gorgeousness fried her neurons or made them work backwards so only half coherent verbal diarrhea just spewed from her mouth.

Ethan gave her half a grin, amused for some reason.

"You should really put a shirt on," Chloe blurted out, then spun on her heels and raced down the hall.

8

Ethan

ETHAN WATCHED Chloe run down the hall and disappear downstairs, but the feel of her in his arms lingered. The impression of her soft cheek against his chest had immediately erased any anger that had remained toward his brother. And her glasses completely obliterated the similarities between Chloe and Margot from Ethan's mind. He wished she'd wear them all the time.

The sisters might be alike at first glance but the more time he spent with Chloe, the more Ethan began to see the subtle differences. There was also the obvious. Chloe was shorter and curvier with beautiful full lips and the perfect hourglass figure. Ethan preferred girls like that as opposed to Margot's rail-thin frame. And Chloe smelled like sugar cookies. That was way better than Margot's overpowering perfume of the week. Chloe's hazel eyes were lighter than her sister's and the warm glow of the white

Christmas lights in the hall had illuminated the gold flecks that shimmered in Chloe's green-brown irises. But perhaps the most interesting difference in Chloe was the way she made Ethan feel.

Unlike Owen, Ethan didn't let himself fall for every pretty girl who batted her eyelashes at him. Actually, Ethan didn't date at all. Despite what he said to Owen about not hiding the truth, Ethan hated the idea of letting someone close enough to see just how messed up he was. Plus, he didn't see the advantage of getting attached to people. All that did was give them the potential to one day hurt him.

Yet, there was something about Chloe that drew him in and made him want to drop all his defenses. She had this soft, vulnerable aura that surrounded her, inviting him in, even when her words didn't. So when his feet carried him to follow her downstairs instead of back to his bedroom, he wasn't that surprised.

Chloe

Chloe was standing in the kitchen, stirring hot vanilla soy milk into her gingerbread hot cocoa mix when she felt Ethan's presence behind her. She didn't know how she knew it was him, but she did. And she hated the way the thought of him made her heart race.

"That smells good," he said. "Got enough for one more?"

She sighed, reminding herself to be a gracious host. Her mother would kill her if she were anything but polite to Margot's friends. And honestly, making Ethan a cup of hot cocoa was the least Chloe could do after insulting him at dinner, tackling him in the hall and then assuming he was flirting with her.

"Sure," she replied, pulling another ceramic mug from the cabinet.

Chloe rolled her eyes realizing the mug was one she'd made when she was in elementary school. It had her name painted above a snowman face with a sloppy red and green handle that was meant to be his scarf. She shouldn't be surprised. They only had Christmas mugs in her house. *Just one more perk of living Christmas every day of her life.*

The Christmas craziness of her home and life was the norm for Chloe, but from the way Ethan gawked at her family's overdone decorations, it was obvious this was far outside his comfort zone. She thought about looking for a less Christmas-y mug for him, but rummaging around in the cupboard for a new mug would only make it seem like Chloe cared—*which she didn't.*

So Chloe filled the embarrassing snowman mug with hot cocoa and handed it to Ethan, determined to keep her winter break plans of healing her broken heart—*which would never happen if she fell for the gorgeous college boy standing shirtless in her kitchen.* She was through with boys and all the drama they brought to her life. *At least she wanted to be . . . but the way Ethan stared at her sure made it difficult.*

"Aren't you cold?" she asked.

"Actually, I'm freezing. I'm not sure I packed appropriately for this weather."

Chloe smirked, finding it hard to believe Ethan hadn't brought at least a t-shirt. "Where did you think you were going, Barbados?"

"Bermuda, actually."

"What?"

"I was supposed to be on an island right about now sipping daiquiris until my brother changed his mind about where we were spending Christmas."

She laughed. "Wow and he chose upstate New York instead? Bad choice."

"It wasn't exactly a choice," Ethan said taking a sip of his hot cocoa. His eyes flashed to hers as he swallowed, filling her with heat. "This tastes amazing, by the way."

"Thanks," Chloe added quietly. She took a sip of her own hot cocoa, trying to forget the way it felt being pinned by his blazing eyes. Instead, she wondered what he'd meant by, *'It wasn't exactly a choice.'*

Maybe Margot had forced the issue. She knew how persuasive her sister was when she wanted something. She glanced at Ethan while taking another sip of cocoa. Maybe he was just as weirded out as she was to be spending Christmas with strangers.

"I'm sorry," she said softly.

"For what?"

"For what I said earlier about your family."

Ethan shrugged. "It's not a big deal."

"No, it kind of is. I'm not usually a jerk, it's just . . ."

"Your sister bringing two strangers home for Christmas royally screwed up your plans?"

She smiled. "For a stranger, you're pretty good at reading my mind."

Ethan gave her that almost-grin of his again and it sent shivers down Chloe's spine. *Shivers he mimicked.*

"Let's get you a shirt," she said walking to the hall closet.

There were sweatshirts, jackets and blankets stuffed in every spare closet of the Price house. In Pine Island you never knew when you'd need one. Smirking to herself, Chloe pulled out one of the many spare ugly Christmas sweaters from the lodge and handed it to Ethan.

He looked at the real jingle bells adorning the light up wreath on the front of the sweater and frowned. "You can't be serious?"

"Do you want to freeze?"

Ethan gave the sweater a shake, making the bells tinkle. Darcy barked at it. "See, even the dog thinks it's hideous."

Chloe laughed. "Darcy just thinks it's a snack. He thinks he can eat everything, isn't that right?" she asked scooping the little dog up.

Ethan took a step closer and scratched the dog's head. "Darcy? As in Mr. Darcy?"

Chloe's eyes widened. "You read Jane Austen?"

"Guilty," he replied.

"Why?"

Ethan huffed a laugh. "Can't a guy just enjoy Austen?"

"No."

He laughed again. "Alright, you got me. Owen's an English major. I read his books when I'm bored."

"Shut up!" Chloe exclaimed. "That's what I wanted to be."

"Wanted to be?"

Embarrassment prickled Chloe's skin. "Yeah. I decided it wasn't a very practical major. I'm going for nursing instead. Or at least I will be next fall."

"Really? Where are you going?"

"Columbia."

Ethan's dark eyebrows rose. "Impressive."

"Thanks, I know," she replied sarcastically. "I'm also graduating top of my class, with my AA so I'll actually be taking junior level courses next year." Chloe bent down to place the dog on the floor and give him a treat. When she stood up she asked, "Where do you go to college?"

Ethan's steady eyes met hers. "Columbia. I'm a freshman."

Chloe's heart skipped a beat. *Did he just say Columbia? Would she be at the same school as him next year?* She couldn't fight the giddy excitement that suddenly welled up inside her.

"What?" he asked, noting the flurry of emotions coursing through her.

"Nothing . . . it's just I realized I'll actually know someone when I start in the fall. But I'll be one year ahead of you, in case you weren't sure."

Ethan

Ethan could barely fight the urge to smile as he caught the teasing tone in Chloe's voice. Now he was even more intrigued by her. The girl was beautiful *and* smart. Plus, she liked the classics enough to name her dog after one.

He secretly adored them, but he felt declaring himself an English major would be following in his brother's footsteps too closely. Besides, he really wasn't sure that's what he wanted to do with his life. Actually, nothing really interested him enough to choose a career path. He was sort of just limping along, undeclared.

Owen was right. Ethan did need to try to find something to make life enjoyable. But that was easier said than done. He glanced at Chloe again. *What do you say, Chloe? Are you something I'd enjoy?*

The thought entered Ethan's head so swiftly it surprised him. *What the hell was he thinking?*

Ethan tried to clear his head. The last thing he needed was to get involved with Margot's sister. But he couldn't deny that there was something about Chloe he was drawn to. *Maybe a little flirting wouldn't be the worst thing in the world?*

A silence had settled over them and Ethan realized he was staring. He put his mug of cocoa on the counter and sighed looking at the little dog. "She's gonna make me wear this isn't she, Darcy?"

The dog cocked his head to the side as if he was trying to

understand and Chloe smirked, reaching for the hideous sweater Ethan held. "I can get you something different."

Ethan pulled it out of her reach. "Oh, I see how it is. Once you know someone shares your taste in books they don't have to wear the ugly sweaters?"

She laughed and a coy smirk lifted one corner of her perfect lips. "Maybe."

"That's rather snobbish, Chloe, " he teased.

She rolled her eyes and tried to tug the sweater from him. "Maybe I'm a snob."

Ethan didn't let go. "I think you are." He tugged the sweater back toward him, pulling Chloe with it. "But I think I'm kinda attached to this hideous sweater now."

"Suit yourself," she whispered. But the teasing tone had left her voice and Ethan couldn't help noticing how close her lips were to his. All he'd have to do is bend down another inch or two . . .

What are you doing to me, Chloe?

Chloe

CHLOE WAS PRETTY sure she'd forgotten how to breathe. She'd definitely forgotten why she was holding onto the ugly Christmas sweater that was balled up between her and Ethan. If it weren't there she'd be pressed against his toned chest again.

She couldn't help glancing longingly at the slight tan that kissed every inch of his skin. Heat blossomed all over her, like the sun was somehow contained in Ethan's veins. Chloe followed the long, lean lines of his arms all the way up to his perfectly chiseled face.

Ethan was obscenely beautiful. Chloe knew boys preferred to be called handsome, but she didn't care. That word wasn't exquisite enough to define Ethan's superb features. From the obsidian of his hair to the emerald shade of his eyes to the dark fringe of lashes to the tiny scar on his chin—*all of it was perfection.*

It wasn't fair, really. *How was a girl to resist?* But she had to. *Right?*

If she gave in to this momentary attraction drawing her near, Chloe would only end up breaking her barely healed heart all over again. And that was not her intention.

As if he knew she was about to pull away, Ethan released his hold on the sweater. The jingle bells rang like tiny alarms, telling her to run.

Nothing good can come from kissing this boy, Chloe.

But as Ethan looked down at her with the same longing in his eyes that she felt in her bones, Chloe changed her mind. Without even knowing she'd made the decision, her body rushed forward until her lips met his.

The kiss was fast and electric, and though the taste of sugar and spice from their cocoa burned its way into Chloe's mind, it couldn't scorch away all the reasons she shouldn't be kissing a shirtless college boy in her kitchen right now.

She pulled away, stopping their kiss as suddenly as it had started. Her hand flew to her lips. "Sorry," she whispered. "I shouldn't have done that."

Ethan reached toward her but she leapt away, shouting a hurried, "I'm sorry," over her shoulder as she ran out of the kitchen and back to her bedroom with Darcy hot on her heels.

9

hloe

December 23rd

Dear Journal,
I kissed a boy last night.
A boy who isn't Brady.

Ethan

Ethan lay in the tiny twin bed in Margot's bedroom. Owen slept next to him, snoring loud enough to wake the dead. Dawn was breaking and Ethan had yet to fall asleep. He couldn't stop reliving Chloe's unexpected kiss and then her even more unexpected departure.

That kiss had been perfect, probably the best of his life, until she pulled away from him like he had herpes. *He didn't.* No tongue rings or braces or any other oddity that would've warranted such a response. He couldn't figure out what he'd done wrong and it was driving him crazy.

He'd even made sure he hadn't been the one to make the first move. *Chloe had kissed him!* It might not have been so maddening if he didn't have to sleep in the room so close to hers for the next week or maybe if that kiss hadn't woken a longing inside him that he'd never felt before. Ethan had to repeatedly fight the urge to walk across the hall, knock on her door and demand to know what the hell kind of game she was playing.

You're killing me, Chloe. I don't need this in my life.

It wasn't like Ethan hadn't kissed girls before. He was acutely aware of how attractive he was. It was hard to miss when he had Owen to stare at. They were almost mirror images of each other. Owen was just a bit taller and more broad-chested. But that was because he had three years on him. But attention from women was nothing new. Ethan had been getting attention from girls since the summer he got his braces off and hit a growth spurt that still hadn't stopped.

At six-foot-three and with a family history of wealth far beyond normal means, it was easy for Ethan to get girls when he wanted to. In the past Ethan's hook-ups had always been casual. But with Chloe it felt different. He barely knew a thing about her, yet he felt a deep connection to her the moment he laid eyes on her. He swore she felt it too. He saw it in her eyes. And that kiss. There was nothing casual about the way that kiss had made Ethan feel.

So why did you run, Chloe?

He ran his hand through his thick black hair in frustration. *Did the Price sisters have some sort of pact to drive him crazy?*

Ethan glanced at his brother who was sleeping soundly. It sucked that Ethan couldn't even talk to Owen about this. His brother would probably kill him if he admitted he kissed Chloe after all the grief Ethan had given Owen about Margot.

Ethan's feelings for Chloe certainly didn't give him a leg to stand on when it came to complaining about Margot. If this was the way Margot made Owen feel it wasn't any wonder why he followed her around like a lost puppy.

Ethan shook his head in disgust at his own churning emotions. This was why he didn't date. Punching his pillow, he rolled onto his side and closed his eyes determined to get at least an hour of sleep before being plunged back into this Christmas nightmare.

10

Chloe

Chloe had never felt so uncomfortable in her own house before. Breakfast, which was usually a simple bowl of oatmeal, had turned into a gourmet affair. Her father was making pancakes in the shape of poorly crafted Christmas icons, while her mother piled plates of bacon, grits and cinnamon buns on the table.

They were really pulling out all the stops for the Hall boys. And had it not been for Chloe's awkward moment with Ethan last night, she would've been ecstatic about the breakfast spread. But as it was, she could hardly keep her orange juice down. Her stomach was in knots as she sat next to Ethan at the table.

She was perched on the edge of her chair as far away from him as possible, but it didn't really help. Even if he were ten feet across the room she'd still feel his presence. Every time she closed her eyes she felt his lips pressed against hers. *Which was precisely why she got no sleep last night.*

She'd tried writing in her journal, but recounting the kiss had made her even more jittery. Even her favorite novels hadn't been able to distract her. *How could they?* She'd just experienced the best kiss of her life. Nothing on paper could ever compare.

Strangely, kissing Ethan had helped reconcile Chloe's pain over getting dumped by Brady. Because never in the entirety of their summer full of kissing had Brady ever made Chloe feel like Ethan had. *Was it just because Ethan was new and exciting? Or was it something more?*

With the way Chloe was acting, she'd never find out. She jumped every time someone said her name. Ethan probably thought she was crazy, but Chloe had convinced herself someone was going to find out she'd kissed him last night.

Things only got worse when her hand accidentally brushed Ethan's as they reached for the syrup at the same time. She pulled her hand away so quickly she knocked the whole jar of syrup over on top of his plate.

"Omigod! I'm so sorry," she said, jumping up to grab a napkin at the same time he did.

They banged heads and for a moment, Chloe saw stars, but a loud bang brought her focus back. In her fumbled attempt to steady herself she'd put her hand in Ethan's plate and knocked the entire thing onto the floor.

Darcy was in his glory as his little tail swished back and forth while he lapped up bacon, eggs and pancakes like a furry hoover.

"Geez," Margot teased. "You two are one stooge short of a whole act."

Everyone at the table thought Chloe's uncharacteristic Calamity Jane act was hilarious. *Everyone but Chloe.* Laughter chorused around the kitchen as she felt her cheeks heat, which meant they were probably glowing atomic red about now. To make matters worse, Ethan was still standing by her side.

"Are you okay?" he asked softly, his hand brushing her elbow as it slowly traveled up her arm.

"I'm fine," she said, hurriedly taking a step back before he could touch the throbbing spot on her forehead.

"Stop moving," her mother warned as Chloe stepped in a glob of syrup Darcy hadn't gotten to yet. "Here," she said laying a series of dishtowels on the floor. "Socks and slippers off you two. Follow the towels to the living room. Margot, get them some ice packs, will you?"

"Mom, I don't need an ice pack," Chloe argued.

"Sweetie, I can see the goose egg forming already. If you don't want a big red lump for the party, you'd better use the icepack."

Chloe glanced at Ethan. His forehead was barely red. He stuffed his hands in the pockets of his university sweats. "I've got a hard head," he replied, reading Chloe's mind again.

"To the couch, both of you," Chloe's mother ordered.

Knowing arguing would only prolong the awkwardness, Chloe slipped out of her sticky slippers, grateful she at least hadn't been wearing her favorite toasty cocoa pair, and followed the towel trail out of the kitchen.

Ethan

Ethan watched Chloe from the corner of his eye. They each held a frozen icepack wrapped in a holiday dishcloth against their foreheads. Chloe's head was back against the couch, her bright eyes closed. Ethan wished she would open them. Her eyes made her easier to read.

Last night, he'd realized that was another difference

between Chloe and Margot. When Chloe looked at him everything she was feeling was written in her gorgeous hazel eyes. It was like each fleck of gold held a secret and Ethan found himself desperate to learn them all.

That's why it'd been driving him nuts that Chloe wouldn't look at him at breakfast. He'd only gotten one brief glance when she walked into the kitchen and it said everything he feared. *She regretted last night.*

He'd been trying to catch her eye all morning, but she wouldn't even look at him. Which was probably what led to the syrup catastrophe that landed them in this situation.

Ethan couldn't help feeling like a toddler in time out. The feeling was foreign, yet strangely amusing. The entire morning had been, actually. He'd always wished he'd been a part of a normal family that had big messy meals—*a family full of love and laughter.*

That hadn't been the case in his house. Even before the cancer, his parents hadn't been the open or affectionate kind. They'd always been more concerned with appearances.

Ethan sighed, adjusting the hideous holiday dishcloth. A fat Santa Claus riding a reindeer had been embroidered onto it. He couldn't help the smirk that tugged at his normally stoic lips when he looked at it. His parents would've never had something so tacky in their home. But that only made Ethan love it more. In fact, he loved all the over-the-top Christmas decorations in the Price home. It was hard not to stare at them.

He wondered which handmade ornaments and trinkets that adorned the three Christmas trees had been made by Chloe. He was dying for clues as to what had made her the irresistible girl he now found himself so desperate to know. He also wondered how long it took to pack all of this stuff up after the holidays. And where the hell did they keep it all? From what he could tell, the tiny log cabin didn't have more than the few rooms he'd seen. He found himself wondering a lot of things and when he looked at Chloe he couldn't help asking the current question that was on his mind.

"So," he said, causing her to open those gorgeous hazel eyes. "When's the party?"

"Huh?"

"Your mother said you don't want a big lump on your head for the party."

"She means the Christmas Eve party," Margot replied, walking into the living room with Owen by her side.

They sat in the plaid loveseat together, Margot curling her legs up as she snuggled on Owen's lap.

"You never told me about a Christmas Eve party," Owen said.

"That's because I wanted it to be a surprise," Margot said, rubbing her nose against his like they were bunnies.

The ridiculous display of affection made Ethan frown and turn his attention back to Chloe. He wanted to talk to her, not Margot and Owen.

"Not everyone likes surprises," Chloe muttered.

Ethan furrowed his brow. *Was she talking about him and their surprising kiss last night?* If she would just look at him . . . He tried again. "So this party . . . Who's going?"

Again Margot answered for her sister. "Everyone!"

Ethan raised his eyebrows still staring directly at Chloe.

Seeming to sense he wasn't giving up until she answered, she sighed deeply. "My parents throw a party every year on Christmas Eve for family, friends and employees that work at the tree farm and lodge all season. It's kind of a 'we survived the holidays' party."

"It's so much fun," Margot exclaimed. "There's a band and dancing and karaoke and food and my favorite . . . mistletoe!" She swiped a bough of the green-leaved parasitic plant from the basket of cinnamon scented pinecones next to her chair and dangled it above Owen until he kissed her.

Seeing Margot was finally occupied, Ethan turned back to Chloe. "And you're going to this party?" he asked quietly.

"Of course she is!" Margot called. "Oh, and you guys will finally get to meet her boyfriend!"

Ethan's heart thumped to a stop. *Boyfriend?* His eyes met Chloe's.

You have some explaining to do, Chloe.

Chloe

"Where is Brady anyway?" Margot interrupted, getting to her feet. "Is he coming with us to pick out a tree today?"

"No," Chloe said, standing quickly and pulling the icepack from her head. She scanned the room ready to make her escape. She'd waited months to have this discussion with Margot, but funny enough, Brady was the last thing Chloe wanted to talk about right now. She didn't want to have this conversation in front of Owen and Ethan. Especially Ethan, who was looking at her with those piercing green eyes of his and an inquisitive frown that made her want to kiss him again until he gave her that rare, almost-smile.

But Margot wouldn't let it go. "Oh, no! Does he have practice today or something?"

Chloe shrugged. "I wouldn't know."

Margot frowned. "What do you mean?"

"I mean I don't know what he's doing today."

"Why not?" Margot asked.

Chloe's emotions were too close to the surface and she couldn't keep them bottled up anymore, not with Margot's questioning poking holes in the fragile dam keeping Chloe's tears at bay. She wanted to escape to her bedroom, but Margot was moving toward Chloe, blocking the stairs.

"Chloe, what's going on?" Margot asked. "Is everything okay with Brady?"

"You'll have to ask him."

"Why?"

"Because we broke up, okay?" Chloe shouted, shoving past her sister and dashing up the stairs.

ETHAN

ETHAN KNEW it was a terrible reaction, but the moment those words left Chloe's mouth he felt a smile slip into place. *'We broke up.'*

I knew you weren't too good to be true, Chloe.

11

Chloe

CHLOE WAS HUGGING a pillow face down on her bed when Margot knocked lightly on the bedroom door. Chloe didn't look up but she knew it was her sister from the subtle way the mattress moved when Margot's thin frame joined her on the bed.

She began to stroke her hair. "Co-Co, why didn't you tell me?" Margot asked softly.

"I didn't know how," Chloe mumbled into the pillow.

"What happened?"

She shrugged. "I don't know. He decided he liked Maci better, I guess."

"Maci Martin?"

Chloe rolled over and sat up. This had been the part she was dreading, but there was no sense avoiding the truth now.

Margot would just keep digging until Chloe spilled all the details. "Yeah, Maci Martin."

Margot's pretty features reddened defensively. She was going into protective big-sister-mode. "Explain."

Chloe sighed. "I saw them making out at Brady's locker and that was it. We just broke up. Or rather he told me he was with Maci so that pretty much ended things with us."

"What?" Margot was on her feet. "He cheated on you?"

Tears silently made their way down Chloe's cheeks. All she could do was nod.

"Right before Christmas? What a jerk!"

Here it was. The lie she'd been keeping for all this time. "No. Not right before Christmas. It happened three months ago," Chloe whispered. "I haven't spoken to him since."

Margot's anger deflated instantly and she sank back onto the bed, pulling Chloe into her arms. "Oh my God, Chloe. I'm so sorry."

That wasn't the reaction Chloe had been expecting at all. She thought her big sister would be mad that she'd kept the truth from her, but Margot's compassion only made Chloe cry harder. *Why had she kept this from her sister?*

All this time she could've been crying on Margot's shoulder instead of suffering alone.

"I should've been there for you," Margot whispered, wiping tears from both their eyes now.

"It's not your fault, Go-Go. I didn't tell you."

Margot tucked Chloe's hair back behind her ears. "Why didn't you?"

Chloe shrugged. "I was embarrassed. And every time we talked you had something amazing to share. I didn't want to bring you down by talking about my complete and utter failure."

"Chloe, first of all, you didn't fail. This isn't your fault. Brady is a total slime-ball to do that to you. And secondly, I want to know everything that happens in your life. We're sisters."

"I know."

Margot took a deep breath. "I want us to be there for each other in the good times and the difficult times."

"Me too," Chloe said. "I'm sorry I kept this from you."

"It's okay. Just promise you won't shut me out. I need you in my life, Co-Co. More than you know. I love you and I miss this so much," she said stroking Chloe's hair again. "Just having someone to confide in, ya know?"

Chloe nodded. She did know. But it wasn't like Margot to get so sappy. "Is everything okay, Go-Go?"

Margot smiled, tightly. "I think it will be." She took a deep breath and blew it out, regaining her composure. She squeezed Chloe's hand. "I don't think you have any idea how much you mean to me."

"You mean the world to me, too. I've been lost without you this year."

Margot stroked her cheek. "Are you kidding? You've never needed me. You're brilliant and strong and you don't let boys rule your life. You're everything I wanna be when I grow up."

Chloe swallowed hard. That was an incredible compliment coming from her big sister. There was no way Chloe was admitting she'd kissed Ethan now. Honestly, she was beginning to think maybe she dreamt the whole thing up. Kissing boys in her kitchen at midnight was not something she normally did. It just went to show that this whole Brady-situation was making her crazy. Maybe now that she'd told Margot the truth things would go back to normal. She could heal and move on.

"So how have you been dealing with seeing Brady all this time?" Margot asked.

"Not well. He's still dating Maci so I pretty much try to avoid them. I was doing okay until yesterday when I ran into him in the hall."

"What happened?"

"Nothing really. He told me he didn't want things to be weird between us, but then Maci showed up. She doesn't like me talking to Brady so I left."

"That jerk!" Margot hissed. "When I see him I'm gonna give him a piece of my mind."

"Please don't," Chloe begged.

"Why not? No one gets away with hurting my little sister."

"I just want to get over him already," Chloe muttered.

Margot studied her carefully. "Do you?"

"What do you mean?"

"Are you ready to let him go so easily, Chloe? I know how long you had a crush on him. And you two seemed so solid this summer before I left for school. Maybe Maci is the one creating the problem."

Chloe felt her heart constrict painfully. Things *had* been wonderful over the summer. She missed that so much. But she didn't want Brady back—*did she? Was that why she was still having so much trouble moving on?*

"If you want to get him back, I'll help you." Margot got that mischievous sparkle in her eyes. "It can be our Christmas project!"

Chloe's mind snapped back to Ethan and the perfect kiss they'd shared. "I don't know what I want, Go-Go."

Margot pulled her close and gave her a tight squeeze. "Well, I know I want to see my favorite sister happy this Christmas."

Chloe grinned. "I'm you're only sister."

"Even if I had a hundred sisters, you'd still be my favorite, Co-Co."

Tears sprang to Chloe's eyes as she hugged her sister back. "I've missed you, Margot."

"I've missed you, too." Margot pulled back after squeezing Chloe just the right amount. "You don't have to have it all figured out, you know? With Brady, I mean."

Chloe frowned. "But I want to. I hate feeling like this. I want everything to be perfect and easy, like it is with you and Owen."

Margot laughed. "We're far from perfect, Chloe."

"But you guys look so happy. And you said you love him."

"I do. But that doesn't mean I have everything all worked out." Margot twisted her hands in her lap, looking anxious. "I know he misses his family. That's why I wanted to bring him here for Christmas . . . to make things better." She frowned again and her voice trembled. "But I think I'm making things worse."

"How?"

Margot sucked in another steadying breath and plastered on a smile. "It's nothing for you to worry about."

"But you're my sister. I want to help if I can."

Margot took Chloe's hand and pulled her off the bed. "This particular issue can wait. Right now, we need to do what we do best."

"What's that?" Chloe asked.

"Spread some Christmas cheer."

ETHAN

MARGOT HAD FOLLOWED Chloe upstairs about twenty minutes ago and it was driving Ethan crazy not being able to hear their conversation.

"Did you know she had a boyfriend?" Ethan asked.

Owen stuffed his hands in his pockets as he leaned against the banister and nodded. "Of course."

"Well, thanks for telling me."

"I'm pretty sure you were there when Margot mentioned it. She talks about Chloe all the time. Maybe if you listened to her every once in a while . . ."

Ethan rolled his eyes. "The girl talks twenty-four-seven, Owen. You can't seriously expect me to listen to every nonsensical thing that comes out of her mouth. Last week she talked about types of braids for an hour."

Owen shrugged. "Well, if you're interested in her sister maybe you should listen."

Ethan stopped pacing and glared at his brother. "Who says I'm interested in Chloe?"

Owen's lips pulled into an easy smile. "I'm not blind, brother. It's pretty easy to see."

"What's easy to see?" Ethan pushed.

"That you're into her."

Ethan scoffed. "You're wrong."

"Whatever you say, E."

The sound of Chloe's bedroom door opening stole the reply Ethan had been readying. He walked over to join his brother at the stairs and watched the girls descend. They'd both changed into warm winter sweaters and leggings. Margot's hair was braided—*of course*—while Chloe's was still in a messy bun. Her creamy skin was blotched with color and her beautiful eyes were red-rimmed and puffy. She was trying to hide it with her smile, but she'd been crying.

Were you crying over him, Chloe?

Ethan balled his hands into fists and cracked his knuckles. He was surprised by the protective feeling that flared in his chest when he thought of someone making her cry. He already hated this Brady kid. Ethan found himself hoping he'd come to the Christmas Eve party so he could tell him exactly what he thought of him.

"So," Margot said, cheerfully. "You guys up for decorating a Christmas tree?"

Ethan glanced at the large, fully decorated trees in the living room, then back at Margot. "You already have three Christmas trees."

Margot laughed. “It’s not for us, silly. It’s for the lodge.”

Just then Mr. Price marched into the living room with an axe. “You kids ready to go get our tree?”

“Where?” Ethan asked.

Mr. Price grinned. “Out there,” he said pointing toward the door.

“We cut our own trees,” Margot said proudly.

Owen laughed. “Awesome!”

“Are you serious?” Ethan asked.

“Deadly,” Mr. Price said.

“Tom takes his Christmas trees very seriously,” his wife said, coming into the room with a large thermos. “He’s been growing them since before the girls were born.” She leaned in and kissed her husband on the cheek. “Pick a good one, dear.” Then she turned back to the kitchen. “I’ll have lunch ready at the lodge when you get back.”

Ethan’s eyebrows rose. “So we’re gonna go out there, in all that snow, to cut down a Christmas tree?”

“Why not?” Owen replied. “Sounds like a real Christmas adventure.”

“That’s the spirit!” Mr. Price said.

“But we didn’t pack anything warm,” Ethan argued.

“Nonsense. We’ve got plenty of extra winter gear.”

Chloe

Chloe glanced from her father to Ethan, her eyes full of alarm as her father opened the coat closet next to the kitchen and began to pull things out. “Dad, they don’t want to wear our old hats and gloves.”

“Sure we do,” Owen replied, tugging a fur-lined trapper hat onto his head. He found another one with a pink plaid pattern and tossed it at Ethan. "Pink is your color, bro."

Ethan handed it to Chloe. Her father started pulling out jackets and sweaters. Then he handed Ethan the same sweater she'd been teasing him with last night. Seeing him hold it again turned her stomach into a tornado of nerves.

Ethan gave her a half-smirk as he examined the familiar sweater. "I couldn't have picked a better one," he said, looking at Chloe.

"You don't have to wear that," she said.

"I want to." He held it up to his nose and sniffed. "It reminds me of hot cocoa at midnight."

Chloe felt her cheeks heat. *God, his voice . . . and the way he smirked at her with only one side of his delicious lips . . .* It made her legs feel like jelly. He tugged the sweater over his head.

"Are you going to wear one?" he asked Chloe, pointing to the closet full of red sweaters.

"I think I'll stick with this one," she replied, running her hands over the warm knit sleeves of her cream sweater.

"This is going to be so fun!" Margot said, passing out pairs of snowshoes to everyone. "Have you guys ever used these?"

Chloe watched Ethan examine the bindings on the lightweight aluminum cleats.

"Not a lot of use for snowshoes in Manhattan, babe," Owen teased.

"Don't worry, my girls will show you how to use them," Mr. Price said. "Chloe, you show Ethan the ropes," her father said, holding out two pairs of hiking poles.

Chloe reluctantly took them and walked over to Ethan. "You'll want to sit down," she instructed.

Ethan followed her over to the bench in the hallway and took a seat while Chloe knelt in front of him, preparing the snowshoes. Once she had the bindings open she set the snowshoes next to his feet. He was already wearing a pair of borrowed boots.

"Okay," she said, "Watch how I do the bindings on this first one and you can do the second one."

Ethan bent closer so his face was near Chloe's, watching her as she fumbled with the bindings. Normally, she could do this in her sleep, but with Ethan's eyes on her she kept losing focus. When it was his turn to try she helped him hold open the bindings to slip his other boot in. Their fingers brushed and the electric current that swept through her made her gasp out loud.

In that split second, Ethan's eyes met hers. They were a stormy green sea, threatening to drown her. Chloe pulled back knowing two things for certain. She needed to sort out her feelings for Brady, because she could easily fall for Ethan.

Once everyone was dressed and ready, Chloe's father slung on his hiking pack. "Looking good crew. Now let's get hopping so we can make it in before the snow starts."

12

Ethan

"So, chopping down trees is what passes for fun out here?" Ethan asked as he struggled to keep up with Chloe in the clumsy snowshoes.

Chloe gave him a tight smile. "It's weird, I know, but it's our family tradition."

"For the lodge?"

"Sort of. The lodge is new, but the daily tree decorating isn't. My great-great grandfather started it. He would bring in a new tree to the barn every day for the twelve days leading up to Christmas so whoever came to the farm to pick out a tree could add an ornament with a Christmas wish in it to the tree."

"Sounds like a lot of work," Ethan replied.

Chloe huffed a laugh. "It is."

"So why do you do it?"

She shrugged. "My family wants to keep the tradition alive."

"Do you always do what your family wants?"

Ethan could tell Chloe was contemplating the answer from the way she pushed her lips together. He was starting to learn her tells. A little voice in his head told him to leave her alone, but for some reason he couldn't.

He hated that Owen was right, but he was interested in Chloe. There was something intriguing about her. She possessed a quiet, sadness almost equal to the one Ethan constantly felt. Recognizing that feeling in another person comforted him and made him desperate for clues as to what made the irresistible girl tick. Maybe it would help him understand himself better . . . and why he had so much trouble letting himself heal.

Chloe

CHLOE WASN'T sure why Ethan was asking her so many questions. Unless maybe he was just trying to ascertain the level of craziness that ran in her family. He was probably worried about his brother getting serious with Margot when he clearly thought Chloe was crazy. *How could he not after the past few hours they'd spent together?*

Not sure how to answer his latest question, Chloe just shrugged. As if her interactions with Ethan weren't embarrassing enough, Chloe now found herself tromping through the snowdrifts in an old pair of snowshoes with him. She was in Margot's hand-me-down red ski jacket with the fur-lined hood and her black snow pants.

Normally, Chloe didn't care what she wore, but with Ethan by her side she was acutely aware of how unpolished she looked. Especially next to Margot, who was wearing a new fitted black ski jacket and trendy plaid snow pants that fit her like a glove. She had on an adorable gray cable knit hat with a fur pompom on top and matching mittens to complete her perfect look. With her long brown braid and rosy cheeks Margot looked like she could be on the cover of a Christmas card, while Chloe looked more like she'd stolen her mismatched winter hat, scarf and gloves from a thrift store sale bid. *Why hadn't she put a little more effort in?*

Because going after Ethan is hopeless, her inner-voice replied.

It was true. He was a gorgeous college boy and completely out of her league. Even if she raided Margot's closet, he wouldn't want anything to do with Chloe. Especially after the way she'd been behaving. Kissing him at midnight, running away, then practically knocking him out at the breakfast table. And to top it all off she'd blurted out her ex-boyfriend drama in front of him.

No wonder she was single.

Maybe avoiding boys all together was her best plan of action. She obviously wasn't good at figuring them out. She'd thought she'd known Brady, but he'd completely surprised her by cheating. And now Chloe felt even more out of her depth as she tried to figure Ethan out. He kept giving her mixed signals.

The sound of Margot and Owen's laughter filled the frosty air. They were lagging behind as they kissed in the falling snow and fell to the ground as they attempted to make snow angels. Chloe felt jealousy spear her heart like an icicle. It was weird watching her sister make out with a boy that looked so similar to the one Chloe had been kissing last night.

Similar, but not identical, her mind corrected. After only one kiss, Chloe found it easy to notice differences between the brothers. Ethan was slightly shorter and thinner, and he had gray veins of color running through his stormy green eyes. His personality was much different than his brother's, too. Ethan was quieter and more serious than Owen, who was always laughing and smiling.

It wasn't that Ethan was cold, it was just that Owen was so warm it made it seem that way. But Chloe knew how unfair it was to compare siblings. She and Margot shared an extremely close bond, but they were just as different as Ethan and Owen. Despite their looks, she and Margot didn't have a lot in common. Margot was the pretty, outgoing one and Chloe was the smart, shy one. But had they not been sisters, constantly compared to each other, maybe they could've just been Margot and Chloe—without the labels.

Chloe thought about that for a moment, wondering if she might have turned out differently if she hadn't felt there was a clearly defined role for her to fulfill. *Who might she have grown into? Would she have been stronger or better at sticking up for herself if she hadn't always had Margot to lean on?*

"So you really do this every year?" Ethan asked, his voice startling Chloe from her thoughts.

"Yep," she replied, readjusting the sled rope to her other hand.

"Why not just get one from the store?"

Chloe laughed. "Is that what you do in Manhattan?"

"I think that's what people everywhere do," he replied, sarcastically.

"Well, look around you, Manhattan. This is not everywhere."

"You can say that again," he replied, a tiny bit of awe slipping into his voice.

Chloe smiled. It was hard not to see the beauty in her backyard.

Long ago, her father's family had built their home on a two-hundred acre wooded lot. Most of it had been left wild, with copses of massive pines dotting the land around the pond that their home backed up to. But part of it had been plowed and tilled to plant perfect rows of Christmas trees.

Chloe could remember loving the fact that she got to help

her father care for the trees when she was young. They would come out in the summer and mow the rows, pull the weeds, prune the new growth and shear the saplings. It was hard work but it was always worth it come Christmas because she would know exactly which tree she'd want to adorn with ornaments.

She, Margot and Brady would tie red bows with their names on them around the saplings they each thought would be the best. Margot was never right, but Chloe and Brady were usually neck and neck. A sharp pain filled her chest as she thought about Brady. So much had changed.

It felt weird being out here without him. He usually helped pick the trees for the lodge. *Not this year.* This year Brady was on his ski trip with Maci.

Chloe swallowed back the hurt those thoughts evoked and tried to focus on anything else. When Ethan spoke again, she welcomed the distraction.

"Margot was right about a white Christmas," Ethan said.

"That's what you came for, right?" Chloe asked.

"Partially," Ethan replied.

Chloe let his cryptic response slip by and watched the big snowflakes that had begun to fall. "Well, it doesn't get more white than this."

"It's really coming down," Ethan commented coming up along side her.

"Yeah, the forecast said it'll be like this all day and into tomorrow."

"The walk back is going to be brutal in these snowdrifts."

Chloe laughed. "Are you getting tired, city boy?"

"Exhausted," he admitted. "Can't we just cut down one of these?" he asked pointing at the trees they were standing near.

"They're planted in growth order. We always harvest the oldest ones first so they don't get too large."

"Oh. How old are these?" Ethan asked, looking at the four-foot trees they stood next to.

She smiled. "These are only the kindergarteners. We want the teenagers," she replied nodding ahead to where her father was. "We've got a bit more hiking to do," she replied, starting to walk again. "Besides, we want a Scotch pine, not these."

"How can you tell them apart?" Ethan asked, trying to keep up.

"You're kidding, right?"

"They're all tall and green," he said with a shrug.

Chloe stopped walking and grabbed the spikey branch of the nearest tree, holding it out to Ethan. "This is a Colorado blue spruce," she said. "See the short blue needles?"

He nodded.

"They're nothing like the other trees out here and they're really hard to grow, but their color is unique."

She trudged through the blue branches until she came to the next row. "These are the Douglas firs. Their needles are long and soft, but they don't hold up the bigger ornaments very well."

Ethan followed her as she moved to the next row. "These are the Scotch pines. They're my favorite. They are the perfect Christmas tree shape. Some people don't like them because once cut they don't hold their needles as well as the Douglas firs but that never bothered me."

Ethan gave her that crooked, amused half-smirk again.

"What?" she asked, suspiciously.

"You know a lot about trees."

"Just these." Chloe tried not to get caught up in the way Ethan's green eyes sparkled, amplified by the forest of pine trees that surrounded them.

"Why?"

"I used to help my dad with them."

Ethan cocked his head to the side. "Used to?"

Chloe shrugged. "Yeah. It was sort of our thing."

She started walking again as a sudden sadness washed over

her when she realized that she hadn't really enjoyed helping with the trees in a long time. She hadn't intended to stop enjoying it, but ever since the lodge opened, she found herself stuck inside assisting guests more than she liked.

"It's not your thing anymore?" Ethan asked.

Chloe looked to where her father was marching up ahead, axe slung high over his shoulder. She found herself wondering if he missed having her help him out here. Margot wouldn't be caught dead doing manual labor. She preferred working in the lodge, so the Christmas trees had always been Chloe and her father's thing. *Why had she let that get away from her?*

"I guess not," she finally replied.

"Did you just outgrow Christmas or something?"

Chloe rolled her eyes. "You ask a lot of questions, you know that?"

His smirk turned into almost a full smile. "I'm trying to figure you out."

"Well stop," she teased as she stopped walking.

Ethan had been following so close behind her that he crashed into her. His arms went around Chloe's waist but it was too late to stop them both from landing in the snow in a tangled heap thanks to their awkward snowshoes.

Ethan swore, but when he noticed Chloe laughing, he actually huffed a laugh, too. The closest thing she'd seen to a smile flickered across his face so quickly she almost missed it. Chloe noticed Ethan's dimples for the first time. They were breathtaking. Heat flooded her whole body as she wondered what it would be like to make him smile like that more often. Her eyes wandered to his lips. The cold had turned them a rosy red and she longed to kiss them again.

She quickly sat up before she let those sinful lips of his lure her in. Undoing her snowshoes, she climbed to her feet and helped Ethan do the same. Her hat fell off and Ethan picked it up. Before he handed it back, he brushed his chilly fingers across the bump on her forehead.

"Does this hurt?" he asked softly, his face much too close to hers.

She couldn't think of a response with his lips so near hers. For some reason, even though it didn't hurt, she nodded. Chloe couldn't feel the bump—she couldn't feel anything but Ethan's fingers against her skin.

"I'm sorry," he murmured, tucking her snow-damp hair behind her ears.

Chloe shivered. "Your hands are freezing."

She ungloved her own toasty warm hands and pressed his fingers between them. Ethan's green eyes locked on hers when she brought his hand up to her lips and blew hot air over his fingertips. It was a natural reaction. Something her parents had done to her a million times after a day playing in the cold. But from the look Ethan gave her it was the most intimate gesture he'd ever received.

His eyes flared brighter than when she'd kissed him and for a moment, Chloe forgot how to breathe. But then she remembered why she was holding his fingers between her palms and blew warm air onto them again. "Better?" she asked.

Ethan

Ethan nodded, slowly. "Perfect." That was the only way to describe the feeling of having his fingers so close to Chloe's irresistible lips—*absolute perfection.*

God, this girl just did something to him. She disarmed him in the best way possible. He wanted to let her in. He wanted to tell her everything and still have her look at him the way she did now. But that would never happen. That just wasn't how the world worked for Ethan. It was why Owen had girlfriends and Ethan didn't.

Owen was good at keeping their past locked up, but Ethan always ruined things by letting it out. Even now he found himself wanting to blurt out the truth.

He gazed into Chloe's big hazel eyes as she blew her abundant warmth over his fingertips. *How could he explain to her that no one had ever shown him such a simple kindness? And how could he be so close to her without wanting to kiss her again?*

But he shouldn't—*for so many reasons.*

- She was his brother's girlfriend's sister.
- She was only in high school.
- He'd probably never see her again after Christmas.
- And lastly . . .

Ethan stared into Chloe's gorgeous face and forgot what the last reason was. He forgot all the reasons he'd just listed for not kissing her. He knew it was a risk he shouldn't take but he just couldn't stop himself.

Chloe slowly released his hands. Without her holding them Ethan let his fingers inch along her jaw until the warm apples of her cheeks rested in each of his palms. Ethan let his thumb drowsily caress Chloe's lower lip. A breath of steam escaped her mouth but before it could dissipate into the frigid air Ethan captured it with a kiss.

For one bliss-filled moment there was nothing but the sound of snow and his beating heart as Chloe kissed him back. But the moment was over almost as quickly as it had begun.

Chloe pulled away, gasping as she stumbled in the snow.

"Wait," Ethan called chasing after her. He caught her arm and pulled her back to him. "Why do you do that? Why do you run when I know you want this, too?"

"Because I shouldn't be kissing you," she whispered.

"Why not?"

"Because!"

"Because why? I know you don't have a boyfriend."

Chloe's cheeks turned red. "I don't but . . . it's complicated."

For a moment, unwarranted jealousy seized Ethan's heart. "Why? Are you not over him?"

"No. Yes. I mean . . ." Chloe's cheeks turned redder. "I don't know anymore."

Ethan took a deep breath and blew it out watching the cloud of steam float away along with his hopes. "So maybe we shouldn't kiss anymore until you know how you feel."

"Yeah," Chloe said, softly. "I think that's probably a good idea."

Ethan nodded and jammed his gloves back on his hands feeling an icy chill that had nothing to do with the weather come over him. "It's a shame though."

"What?"

"To waste such perfectly matched lips."

He watched Chloe's throat bob as she swallowed thickly. *She felt it, too. He knew it.* Ethan realized he was still holding onto Chloe's hat. "Here," he said handing it back to her. "I think this belongs to you."

"I'm sorry," Chloe whispered, as if she knew he was speaking about his heart rather than the old hat.

"Me too," he replied, his hand catching her arm. "I know it's not my place and I don't even know him, but I can already tell you can do much better than this Brady-guy. You deserve to be with someone who's positive about their feelings for you." Then he let go and walked away.

Chloe

. . .

Chloe stood in stunned silence as she watched Ethan walk away, his words and kiss replaying in her mind. *What on earth just happened? And what had he meant? Had Ethan been talking about himself? Did he* like *her?* A million questions crashed through her mind at once. Before Chloe could make sense of any of them, her father's voice boomed from somewhere in the distance. “Found it!”

Chloe looked ahead to where her father was. Ethan turned to look back at her, a stony expression sliding into place. “Let's go cut down the Christmas tree.”

13

Chloe

CHLOE COULDN'T STOP herself from glancing at Ethan as they decorated the Christmas tree with the never-ending line of guests visiting the lodge. Her quick glances through the tree did nothing to help deter her confusing feelings for him.

Each glimpse revealed a new layer of Ethan she found attractive. The quiet storm of his eyes, the way half of his mouth was always turned down as if he expected the world to disappoint him, the slightest hint of stubble along his strong chin, the way his jaw muscles ticked when he was concentrating, the unintentional confidence he exuded. All of it was alluring.

It was hard to tear her eyes away from him. Even now, as he stood politely chatting with a guest who was clearly flirting with him. Chloe found herself wanting to know what he was thinking. Ethan stood patiently with his hands in his pockets almost smiling at the shameless lodge guest. He looked like a million dollars in the cheesy Christmas sweater all the lodge employees wore. Chloe was convinced no one had ever worn that sweater better than Ethan Hall.

Even with the tacky wreath pattern on the front it was impossible to hide his appeal. It made Chloe wonder just where he came from. He was impeccably well-groomed and his confidence bordered on cocky, yet in a sexy way. She'd never met someone like him. Ethan wasn't trying to impress anyone, and that made him even sexier.

What Chloe wouldn't give to feel that much confidence herself.

Maybe if she had that kind of confidence she could do a better job of sorting out her jumbled feelings, because right now her heart was a mess. And when Ethan caught her staring at him his lips completed the frown they were already halfway to. His stormy green eyes dulled before they darted away completely, returning to his polite conversation with the lodge guest.

Guilt knotted Chloe's stomach as she realized she was the cause of that pained expression. It was the same look he'd given her each time she pulled away from his kiss. She hated herself for behaving so immaturely. This was going to be a long holiday if she couldn't find a way to smooth things over with Ethan. *And what if he told Owen?* Owen would surely tell Margot and then Chloe'd be in an even bigger mess.

Sighing, Chloe grabbed a pen and tiny slip of paper from the wish station her parents had set up. She knew it was childish, but she needed as much help as she could get, so she scribbled her Christmas wish down anyway. *'Figure out what I want.'*

She folded up the wish and stuck it inside a clear glass ornament and hung it on the tree. Then, Chloe set her shoulders, determined to make her wish come true.

She was just crossing the room to talk to Ethan when she heard someone calling her name. She turned to see Brady pushing through the wreath-clad double doors to the lodge and her steps faltered.

Brady

Brady spotted Chloe by the new Christmas tree in the lodge. He figured this was where she'd be. He checked her house earlier but no one was home. And with only a few days left until Christmas he knew the Price family would be busy with festivities at their booming hotel.

It was impressive how they'd turned the little Christmas tree farm into a thriving business in such a short time. Brady remembered when he'd first moved to Pine Island and Everett's Tree Farm hadn't been much more than a small barn to grab a cup of hot cocoa or cider in after purchasing a tree. Now there was a gorgeous rustic building that resembled a ski lodge with hotel rooms, banquet halls for weddings, horse-drawn sleighs, crackling double-sided stone fireplaces, a bar and lounge and room for twelve massive Christmas trees scattered throughout the warm three-story lobby.

That's where Chloe was, looking as beautiful as ever with her wild brown hair piled atop her head. She hadn't seen him yet and Brady took the opportunity to take her in. He hadn't really looked at her since they broke up. Guilt kept him from feeling he had the right to feel anything for her after the way he treated her. But now that things with Maci were over, Brady wanted to make things right with Chloe. Even if it meant they'd never be more than friends, he at least owed her a real apology.

As Brady pushed through the glass doubled doors he noticed what had Chloe's attention. It was a tall, dark and surprisingly good-looking stranger. Chloe was watching him like a hungry cat, her muscles coiled. She was just starting to walk toward the stranger when Brady called her name.

Her startled expression made his heart plummet. *It was clear seeing him wasn't a good surprise.*

"Brady? What are you doing here?" she asked.

The stranger, who'd been talking to a guest nearby, craned his neck to follow their conversation. Brady tried to ignore him. "I came to see if you needed help with the Christmas tree. I'm sorry I missed chopping it down but my game ran long."

Chloe just blinked at him with utter shock. "Why are you here?" she finally repeated.

He tried to hold his smile. "I told you. I want to help with the tree." *And apologize for being a total jerk,* he thought, though he'd been hoping to have that conversation in a more private setting.

"But you're supposed to be on the ski trip," Chloe objected.

"Yeah, coach kinda put the kibosh on the ski trip when he planned a tournament the same weekend."

Chloe was still looking at him distrustfully. "What about Maci? I thought she didn't want you talking to me?"

"Well, Maci doesn't tell me what to do anymore."

Chloe's eyes widened. "Did you break up?"

He nodded. "I miss you, Chloe."

Just then Margot walked over, a clone of the Mr. Tall-Dark-and-Handsome by her side. "Well, well, well. Look what the cat dragged in," Margot drawled. "Brady Jones. Have you come to humiliate my sister further? Because let me tell you, that's not going to happen on my watch."

"Margot," Chloe hissed, her tone a quiet warning.

Brady sighed. *This was not how he'd wanted his apology to go.* He knew Margot would go into protective big-sister-mode. She'd always been Chloe's mouthpiece, but right now Brady didn't want to have to talk through Margot. He looked at Chloe. "Can we go somewhere and talk?"

Chloe stumbled to find words. "I-I don't think—"

"Brady!" Mrs. Price's voice rang through the lobby and she came scurrying over to wrap him in a smothering hug. "I thought that was you! I'm so glad to see you around. It's been much too long, sweetheart. Have you come to help decorate the tree?"

"Yes," he replied politely.

"Great," Mrs. Price replied. "Christmas wouldn't be the same without you."

"I agree," Brady said, looking purposefully at Chloe.

"Are you coming to the Christmas Eve party with your parents?" Mrs. Price asked.

Brady smiled, still not taking his eyes off of Chloe. "I wouldn't miss it."

"Oh good. I'm so glad we'll all be together again this Christmas."

"Me too," he replied. "Me too."

14

Chloe

MARGOT PRACTICALLY RIPPED Chloe's arm off pulling her into the ladies room to question her about Brady.

"What's going on, Chloe? I thought you said you two broke up?"

"We did."

"Then what's he doing here giving you the sad puppy dog eyes?"

"He came to tell me that he and Maci broke up."

"What?"

"I'm as surprised as you. I didn't get all the details before Mom showed up. All he said was he had to skip the ski trip because of some basketball tournament and that he's not dating Maci anymore."

"He didn't say anything else?"

"Well, he did say he wanted to help with the Christmas trees and that he missed me."

"Chloe! This is huge. This could be the Christmas miracle you were waiting for."

"What do you mean?"

"I think you're not over Brady and apparently he's not over you either. Why else would he be here?"

"I don't know. Maybe the holidays are just making him nostalgic or something."

"Or maybe he realizes that he made a huge mistake dumping you for someone as shallow as Maci Martin."

Chloe frowned as the sting of rejection resurfaced. "I don't know, Margot. I'm still not even sure I want Brady back."

"Are you kidding me? You've been in love with Brady Jones since you were ten."

“Yeah, but I'm not ten anymore.”

Margot put her hands on her slim hips. “You're telling me you wouldn't take him back if he asked you to be his girlfriend again right now?"

Chloe bit her lip as images of Ethan popped into her mind. She couldn't get those gorgeous green eyes of his out of her head, or the way he smelled, or the taste of his lips or that sad yet hopeful look he'd given her in the pine forest today.

Did she want Brady back? Or did she want a shot with Ethan?

“Co-Co, I know I haven't been here for you so I don't know all the heartache Brady put you through, but I remember how happy you two were together this summer. I've never seen you smile like that. I want that for you again. And Christmas is the perfect time for second chances.”

That was true. “I'm just afraid he'll hurt me again, Go-Go.” A tear slipped down Chloe's cheek. “He broke my heart. And I hate that no matter what happens I'll never be that girl again, the one who can trust with all of her heart, because he's always going to have the broken pieces of it.”

"Then don't be that girl," Margot said softly. "Be this new version of yourself. You can guard your heart and put it out there at the same time. But you can't be afraid to go after what you want, Chloe. And you can't live your life full of regret. You mean too much to me. I won't sit by and watch you be unhappy. If I hadn't been blinded by my own happiness I'd have seen it sooner. You've lost your sparkle, Co-Co."

Chloe laughed. "You were always the one with the sparkle, Go-Go."

Margot swept a strand of hair away from her face, gently. "Trust me, Chloe. You sparkle. And you deserve to be with someone who can see that."

Chloe bit her lip as longing filled her heart. "That's the problem, Go-Go. I think you're the only one who sees it."

Margot pulled her close. "That's not true. We all sparkle in our own way. The key is finding someone who brightens your shine instead of dulls it. If you think Brady might be that person, then give him a second chance. If not, it's okay to move on."

Chloe let Margot's words sink in, hopeful that they would help her figure out the truth hidden in her wounded heart.

Ethan

Ethan watched Chloe follow Margot out of the ladies room. Her eyes were red-rimmed again. He instinctively began popping his knuckles as he watched Chloe walk back over to her ex-boyfriend. *What do you see in him, Chloe?*

It was plain to Ethan that Chloe was way too good for someone like this Brady character. He was wearing a high school varsity jacket and a beanie pulled low over his shaggy hair. He was tall and lanky, not grown into his frame yet. At least he had the good sense to look nervous. Showing up after dumping a girl as amazing as Chloe was a bold move. Though it seemed Brady was a friend of the Price family so maybe that warranted his bravery.

While Margot and Chloe were in the bathroom, their parents and some of the other lodge employees chatted with Brady, talking sports and holiday plans. He seemed relaxed and friendly with everyone. But as soon as Chloe re-emerged he tensed.

It bothered Ethan that he couldn't tell what Chloe and Brady were talking about from his vantage point. He was sitting in a comfortable winged-back leather chair by the roaring fireplace. He wanted to get up and move closer, but Owen was watching him from his spot at the bar where Margot had joined him.

Ethan decided to turn his attention back to his version of a hot toddy. He'd added a generous helping of whiskey to the hot apple cider he'd ordered at the bar when no one was watching. He took a large sip, letting the heat from the alcohol warm him as it burned deep in his chest.

Chloe and Brady had moved out of sight, leaving Ethan with nothing to do but admire the lodge. This place was much more his style. It had expensive furniture, lavish décor and a lively bar. The clientele seemed like people he might see accompanying his mother to high society brunches or charity events.

Ethan ran his finger over the gold foil stamp on the red cocktail napkin that came with his drink. The logo was a diamond shape with log cabin in the center of a large wreath adorning the doors while snowflakes fell from above. The words, *Everett's Christmas Lodge & Tree Farm, Established 1909*, glared back at him.

It was clear there was a lot of family history here. The walls were covered with giant framed photographs of the farm's humble beginnings and Everett Price, the man who started it all. Ethan found himself wondering how different Chloe's family was from his. *Had they married for love rather than money? Had they had children out of choice rather than obligation?* Ethan wondered how different his life might have been had he been raised here with a true sense of family.

It was funny, he was only a few hours away from New York City, yet he felt like he was a world away from everything he knew. Strangely, Ethan didn't think he would miss the money and privilege that came with his upbringing if he had what the Price family had.

Everyone who passed them stopped to say hello or offer kind wishes. Even the staff held an immense amount of love and respect for Mr. and Mrs. Price. He watched in awe as they started to dance in front of the Christmas tree when a familiar Bing Crosby tune began to play. Some of the guests stopped to watch, some joined in. Margot pulled Owen onto the impromptu dance floor. His face was so full of joy it was painful for Ethan to watch. Painful, because he knew he could look that same way if he could only find a way to let himself.

It was impossible watching a near-mirror image of himself, living the life he wanted. One full of happiness and health, while Ethan's own life was consumed with a sorrow that was eating him alive.

He watched as Owen laughed with Margot, spinning her around under the mistletoe, stealing kisses every chance he got. Owen looked like he belonged here with these happy people. Ethan wished he did, but he feared that there was a part of him that would forever remain broken after the loss of his mother and abandonment of his father.

Owen had been through it all alongside Ethan, but it seemed they wore their scars differently. Owen's pain had torn a hole in his heart—a void he was constantly trying to fill with anything that brought him joy, while Ethan's pain festered, hardening into a thick scar tissue that prevented anyone from getting past it.

Sometimes Ethan felt like his entire body was covered in a thick coat of sorrow, making it impossible for him to connect with anyone.

Not Chloe, though. Chloe had somehow slipped past his defenses.

Ethan looked past the massive Christmas tree that she had disappeared behind, wondering for the millionth time what it was about her that he couldn't resist. He despised the anxious feeling that settled in his chest whenever he thought of her.

What are you doing to me, Chloe?

15

Brady

BRADY'S HEART was in his throat when he led Chloe into one of the small ballrooms that wasn't being used. He couldn't believe she'd agreed to talk to him. *What had Margot said to her in the ladies room? Was she on his side after all?*

When Chloe had practically run into the bathroom in tears, Brady hadn't thought he had a chance in hell with Chloe. But now here she was standing next to the baby grand piano in the dark ballroom. A few strands of white lights lit up the rows and rows of white chairs, making her pale skin glow.

"Looks like a wedding," he commented.

Chloe crossed her arms and glared at him. "What do you want, Brady?"

"Okay, so no small talk then . . ."

"You haven't talked to me in months, what did you expect?"

Brady pulled his hat off and ran his hands through his hair.

She was right, he was expecting too much. But he needed to apologize regardless. “I just wanted to tell you that I'm really sorry.”

“About what?” Chloe asked. “Cheating on me, getting caught, dumping me, ignoring me?”

“All of it,” he said, taking a step closer to reach for her hand.

She pulled away. “Brady, this apology is three months too late.”

“You’re right, but I’m apologizing anyway. I was a jerk, okay? And now that I’ve been dumped I’m finally realizing just how terrible I must’ve made you feel.”

Chloe’s mouth fell open. “Maci dumped you?”

He nodded.

“Is that why you’re here?”

“No.” He sighed. “I don’t know. I just know I feel like crap and if I made you feel even an ounce of what I’m feeling right now, I just wanted you to know how sorry I am.”

Chloe

Chloe was silent for a moment contemplating her next words carefully. Brady took her silence as defeat and sat down in one of the chairs, hanging his head.

After a while, Chloe joined him, sitting one chair away. “You did hurt me, Brady,” she said quietly. “A lot.”

He looked up. “I’m sorry, Clo.”

“Me too,” she said.

“What are you sorry for?”

She shrugged. “That you got dumped. I know how bad it sucks.”

He huffed a laugh and shook his head.

“What?”

"I always knew you were too good for me."

"What's that supposed to mean?"

"I came here to apologize because I'm a jerk and you're the one comforting me."

Chloe smiled. "Well, I know I could've used a friend after this jerk I was dating dumped me, so . . ."

Brady grinned that dazzling all-star smile of his. "He sounds like a tool. You shouldn't date tools, Clo."

She gave him a sad smile. "I don't plan to again."

Brady

That comment was sobering to Brady and he felt the humor of the situation evaporate. He looked at Chloe, his tone turning serious. "I really am sorry."

"I know."

"So can we be friends again?" he asked. "I think I could really use one."

Chloe gave him that slow, sweet smile of hers that always melted his heart. "I think I can manage that."

"Good." He gave her another of his flirty smiles. "Wanna bash my ex-girlfriend with me?" he teased.

"Only if you're willing to talk smack about my ex-boyfriend with me."

This time Brady's smile was genuine. "Deal," he said, extending his hand.

Chloe shook it and Brady pulled her into a hug. With her in his arms all his old feelings came rushing back. *It was true what they said. Sometimes you didn't know what you had until you lost it.*

It was going to be difficult for Brady to be just friends with Chloe after they'd been so much more. But if friends was what she was comfortable with, that would work—*for now.*

16

Chloe

When Chloe returned to the lodge, Ethan was nowhere in sight. At first it was a relief. Having his piercing gaze on her constantly made Chloe sweat and she didn't want to have to introduce him to Brady who seemed determined to stick around. But after a while, Chloe was concerned about where Ethan had gone off to.

She found Margot working the snow-cone machine with Owen, who was having way too much fun pumping hot maple syrup onto the fluffy white snowballs.

"Did you see where Ethan went?"

"He said he needed to do some homework," Owen replied.

"Oh." Chloe frowned at the thought of Ethan being alone.

He already seemed like he didn't belong. Maybe all the commotion at the lodge was too much for such a somber soul.

She couldn't really blame him. Every time a classic Christmas song came on her parents started dancing. And there were children running around the various trees in the lobby throwing tinsel at each other. It could be a little much for her sometimes, too.

So she let her worry for Ethan go and busied herself at the lodge for the rest of the afternoon. After the tree was decorated and the last minute arrangements for the wedding were complete, Chloe moved out to the barn to help wrap Christmas trees and load them onto people's cars. Brady was by her side the entire time.

She had to admit it was nice having her friend back. She forgot how much he made her laugh. But by the time she returned to her house for dinner her cheeks hurt from laughing and she was pleasantly exhausted.

"Want to stay for dinner?" Chloe asked.

"I'd love to, but I told my mom I'd be home to watch my brothers tonight."

"Okay. Well, give them my love."

Brady grinned. "I will."

Chloe turned to go inside, but Brady pulled her back. "Hey, can we hang out tomorrow?"

His question caught her off guard. But she didn't know why. *It wasn't like he was asking her on a date.* "Uh, sure. I guess."

"I was thinking we could take the snowmobiles out in the morning."

"Oh, that's a great idea. It'll be fun with all this fresh snow. Can I ask Margot to join?"

"Sure. The more the merrier."

"Okay, see ya in the morning."

"Night," Brady called, waving as he jogged back down the driveway.

. . .

Ethan

Ethan looked up when the door opened. Chloe walked in covered from head to toe in a fine dusting of snow. She looked like a Christmas angel and he was surprised by the tightness he felt in his chest upon her return. *Had he missed her?*

He didn't let himself miss people. Missing them meant he'd have to get attached to them and that was something he wasn't in the habit of doing. All that led to was disappointment, which was the other subtle feeling that crept up on Ethan as he watched Brady disappearing down the drive in the distance.

"Sorry I'm late," Chloe called as she walked into the living room. "Is dinner ready? I'm starving."

"Five more minutes on the cornbread," her mother called from the kitchen.

Ethan closed his book and stood up from his seat by the fire.

Chloe jumped. "Ethan!" Her hand flew to her chest. "I didn't see you there."

"It's where I've been all night," he said, holding up one of his English Literature books.

"Oh. Well, we missed you at the lodge."

"Did you?" he asked accusingly. He was under the impression she was too occupied with Brady to be missing him. *Am I wrong about you, Chloe?*

He didn't get a chance to find out because Margot barged into the living room announcing that dinner was ready.

Chloe

. . .

It was unnerving how quiet Ethan was during dinner. He'd barely said two words as the chili and cornbread were dished out. Now he sat silently stirring his spoon around the bowl, still not taking a bite of it. Owen had almost polished off his bowl already. Chloe glanced at Ethan from beneath her lashes as she took a bite of her own piping hot vegetarian chili. She'd never seen someone look so completely different based on his moods.

Earlier, when they'd been walking in the pine forest, Ethan had looked exuberant, the sparkle in his eyes almost cheerful. And when they'd kissed . . . it was like his face had come alive, the stormy green sea of his eyes transforming into inviting meadows. But now, as he glowered at his bowl of chili, Chloe could practically feel his sadness.

Guilt stabbed at her gut. *Was his sullen mood her fault?* She hoped not. Maybe he just didn't like chili, though she'd never seen someone scowl at a bowl of chili quite like that before.

Taking a chance, Chloe nudged Ethan with her elbow, breaking him from the mesmerizing trance of stirring. "Do you not like chili?" she whispered.

He shrugged. "I've never had it."

Chloe's eyebrows raised. She looked around the table realizing no one else was paying attention to their conversation. Her parents were too busy sharing embarrassing stories about Margot with Owen—*again*.

"You've never had chili?" Chloe whispered.

"That's what I said."

"Is Manhattan too good for chili?" Chloe asked, jokingly. "If so I might seriously have to reconsider my plans to attend college there."

Ethan didn't crack a smile. He just continued staring at the bowl.

"I can't believe your Mom never made you chili! It's the perfect winter meal."

"My mother didn't cook."

Chloe stopped eating. "What? Why not?"

"The kitchen staff prepared all our meals."

She laughed, but when she realized he wasn't joking she felt her throat go dry. *Just who the hell were these boys?* If they had *'kitchen staff'* what the heck were they doing dining with her family around an old dinged up pine table her grandfather had built?

"Well, you've been missing out," she said eating a spoonful of the heavenly chili.

He frowned and shook his head. "I don't think it's for me."

Chloe crossed her arms. "How are you so certain you won't like it if you won't give it a try?" she asked.

Ethan

Ethan's heart skipped a beat as a wave of déjà vu hit him so hard he was speechless. Chloe's words . . . His mother used to say the same thing. Not just a similar phrase, but the exact same wording. *'How are you so certain you won't like your new school if you won't give it a try? How are you so certain you won't like living with your grandmother? How are you so certain I won't beat the cancer?'*

The memories of his mother unexpectedly gripped Ethan, sending a wave of agony through him so swiftly that he thought he might be sick. Chloe put a hand on his arm and he stood abruptly, shoving his chair back with a screech.

Ethan was aware the dinner conversations came to a halt but he didn't care. He muttered a hurried, "Excuse me," and rushed from the table to the sanctuary of the bedroom upstairs.

. . .

Chloe

Chloe realized her mouth was hanging open and she snapped it shut. Embarrassment flooded her. *Was it her fault Ethan had just run from the table?*

She'd thought she was just making light conversation. She certainly didn't mean to offend him.

"Do you need to go check on him?" Margot asked Owen.

He shook his head. "Nah, Ethan gets kind of moody around the holidays. I apologize. It's nothing you did," he said, directing his last comment at Chloe.

She swallowed hard and nodded, but wasn't so sure she believed Owen. No one got that offended about chili for no reason—*holidays or not.*

"So," Margot said changing the subject. "Can we expect to see Brady more over winter break?"

Chloe snapped to attention, hating that her forward sister was bringing Brady up in front of everyone. She needed to take hold of the conversation before Margot started fishing for details of what she and Brady had talked about at the lodge. "Yes. Actually, he's coming by tomorrow morning. He wanted me to ask if anyone wanted to go snowmobiling?"

Owen's face lit up. "No way?! Can we? I've always wanted to try that."

Margot grinned. "Of course. That's a great idea, Chloe. We can all go."

Chloe turned to her father. "As long as you don't need us at the lodge in the morning."

"I think I can spare you for a few hours," her father replied, giving her a wink.

Margot clapped her hands. "Yay!"

The rest of the dinner was filled with stories about snow-mobiling and other outdoor winter activities Owen wanted to try, but Chloe had a hard time focusing. She couldn't stop thinking about Ethan and what could've possibly made him leave the table so abruptly. Normally, her curiosity would make her determined to find out, but there was something about the sadness in Ethan's eyes that made Chloe afraid to dig deeper.

17

Chloe

After dinner Chloe decided to go to her bedroom to work on some homework. She did have schoolwork to do, but it was more of a self-imposed grounding than anything else. She needed to get her emotions under control. She still had no idea why Ethan had left the table. Or what to do about the way kissing him made her feel.

It didn't help that suddenly Brady was back in her life. Sorting out her feelings for one mysterious boy was trouble enough. But now Brady was begging for forgiveness and saying all the things she would've killed to hear three months ago.

Was it too late for them to be anything more than friends? Or was Margot right? Could this Christmas bring second chances?

And what about Ethan?

Everything about him seemed to draw Chloe in. From the moment she'd met him, Ethan had become an all-consuming force. She felt herself being pulled into his web of intrigue, but the closer she got the more tangled her heart felt. Every kiss snared her emotions deeper and if she wasn't careful she'd find herself caught in the web of a boy who may very well take the broken pieces of her heart back to New York City after Christmas.

Was she crazy to even think she had a chance with him?

He'd seemed interested in her in the forest today, but she couldn't understand why. All she'd done was upset him with her questions and indecisiveness.

Chloe sighed and flopped backwards onto her bed. She hugged her, *Read-Sleep-Repeat*, pillow to her chest and closed her eyes willing herself to not think about boys. But it was impossible. The last twenty-four hours had been filled with the two most perfect kisses of her life. The fact that neither of them were with Brady said something that her heart refused to let Chloe ignore.

She wasn't dating Brady anymore, so she shouldn't feel guilty about kissing Ethan, but for some reason she did. Truthfully, Chloe was still confused about her feelings for Brady. But that hadn't been why she stopped kissing Ethan in the pine trees. She'd stopped because she was afraid Margot or her father would catch them at any moment. *Of course that had also been the thing that made the kiss that much more exhilarating.*

Chloe couldn't stop thinking about that kiss. If she had thought the midnight cocoa kiss was amazing then the pine tree forest kiss was epic. It was the thing of romance movies. She could still feel the burn of Ethan's lips against her cold skin. It made her shiver just thinking about it.

God, she was in deep with this boy. Chloe kissed him twice and it felt like he'd somehow erased all common sense. She'd honestly been surprised Ethan had wanted to kiss her a second time after the way she reacted last night. *Who kisses a boy that looks like him and runs away?*

Apparently she did.

"What's wrong with me?" she muttered.

Chloe had been dumped by a boy she'd chased for years and run away from a boy who chased her. And now she had both of them running through her head.

"Just stop thinking about boys," she ordered herself, opening her laptop.

She'd promised herself this winter break was going to be about healing and moving on and that meant she needed to focus on herself, not boys.

Ethan

Ethan glanced at the glowing bedside clock. It was nearly midnight again. He knew a second sleepless night wouldn't bode well for him but he got up anyway. It's not like he could sleep with Owen snoring in his ear.

They'd had another unpleasant conversation when he'd returned from dinner. Ethan shook his head as Owen's words circled back through his mind.

"What did I say about screwing this up for me?" Owen snarled.

"I'm not trying to, but you didn't hear what Chloe said," Ethan argued. "She caught me off guard."

"What did she say?"

"Something Mom used to say."

Owen tensed. "I want you to leave our family drama out of this, E. I mean it. And stop whatever the hell you have going on with Margot's little sister."

"There's nothing going on."

"Good. Keep it that way."

Ethan stared at his brother, sleeping soundly in the tiny bed. *How was it that Owen could sleep so peacefully? Did he really feel nothing? Not even at Christmas?*

Sighing, Ethan pulled on his sweats, grabbed his laptop and headed downstairs. He knew he was being foolish and blatantly ignoring his brother's threats, but he couldn't help hoping that maybe Chloe would be in the kitchen.

He was starving after skipping dinner. He shouldn't have made such a big deal about the chili. And he didn't know why he'd lied to Chloe. He'd had chili before. Only once. On a ski trip his family took to the French Alps. Ethan had been eleven. It was when his mother's illness had first started. She hadn't been diagnosed yet, but she was too sick to ski so Ethan spent most of the trip inside keeping her company. One day she ordered them each a bowl of chili and they ate it together in front of the fireplace. It meant so much to him, cuddling up with his mother for a rare informal meal.

He'd been lost in that memory when Chloe had startled him with her remark. For a moment it was like his mother was still there. It had been a very long time since Ethan felt a connection that strong. It was confusing. On one hand, he missed being able to recall the subtle details of his mother—the things she might say, the way she smelled, the exact shade of her blue eyes. But on the other hand, it was easier letting the memories dull. It made the pain more bearable.

Ethan knew the ache of losing his mother would never go away, but he'd thought he'd learned to live with it. But after spending just a few days with the Price family, he realized he hadn't really been coping at all. He'd been avoiding. Avoiding life. Avoiding connection. Avoiding love.

As he walked into the empty kitchen he couldn't fight the mixture of sadness that filled his chest. Chloe wasn't there. He should be relieved. Owen was right. He shouldn't pursue her. But knowing something and explaining it to his heart were two totally different things.

Although Ethan was hungry, he decided he'd rather starve than be caught snooping around the kitchen. Instead, he settled on the couch and fired up his laptop. The low flames of the dwindling fire still crackled in the hearth. He looked at the clock above the fireplace mantle. In exactly five minutes it would be December twenty-fourth—*the day that changed everything.*

18

hloe

December ~~23~~ 24

Dear Journal,
It's almost Christmas Eve and I'm more confused than ever.
Brady said all the things I've been waiting to hear.
So why am I still thinking of Ethan?

Chloe glanced at the glowing red numbers on her alarm clock. It was two minutes after midnight. Technically that made it December twenty-fourth. It was *already* Christmas Eve. She crossed out the date on her journal entry and corrected it. Sighing, she gave up on writing. She didn't know what to write anyway. Her head and her heart were a mess. The only hope of easing her nerves was downstairs—*hot cocoa.*

ETHAN

ETHAN FROWNED at the glowing lights on the Christmas tree closest to him. He used to love Christmas. Even though his parents weren't as warm and affectionate as the Prices' he'd still enjoyed holidays with his family during his childhood. He had his mother to thank for that. She always took time to make him feel special at Christmas. *Until she got sick.*

His mother was diagnosed with lung cancer on December twenty-third. She'd never even smoked a cigarette. At the age of twelve, Ethan hadn't really understood the significance of that. Or how unfair it was that some people, like his selfish father, smoked daily and remained healthy as a horse, while his mother ended up fighting for every breath.

The doctors told her she wouldn't see another Christmas, but she was determined to prove them wrong. But in the end, they'd been right. His mother took her last breath on Christmas Eve the following year.

It was Christmas Eve again.

Ethan welcomed the ache that came with thinking of his mother. It was the only reminder he had left of her now. And although Ethan promised himself he wouldn't do it this year, he found himself opening his mother's favorite Christmas movie on his laptop. Watching it without Owen made it less meaningful but Ethan's brother had long since outgrown the morbid Christmas Eve tradition.

Ethan had been lying by her side in the hospital bed they'd set up in their Fifth Avenue penthouse with his mother watching, *Miracle on* 34th *Street,* when he realized she felt cold. He pulled her blankets up a little higher. That's when he noticed she wasn't breathing.

He'd only been thirteen.

Taking a deep breath, Ethan focused on the laptop in front of him instead of the suffocating memories. He tried to steady the heavy emotions that threatened to smother him whenever he thought about that night.

Owen had been asleep when their mother died. *Was that why he seemed less scarred now? Because their father had let him sleep through the coroner coming to cart their mother away? Because Owen hadn't felt the cold of her flesh or seen the blue of her lips? Was that why Owen was still whole and Ethan never would be?*

That night had only been the beginning of the nightmare for Ethan. In the years to come he would lose all the family he had in the world—*all except Owen.*

"And that's why I find myself in the middle-of-nowhere for Christmas," Ethan muttered, wiping his eyes with his shirt-sleeves.

He was about to press play on the movie when he heard the stairs creak. He turned around to see Chloe standing there, glasses askew, chestnut hair piled haphazardly atop her head. He couldn't fight the smile that tugged on his lips.

It was impossible for him not to find her attractive. She'd been in the middle of a stretch when she noticed him on the couch and now her hands were frozen above her head. She certainly had the deer in headlights look down.

Damn, am I that terrifying, Chloe?

He guessed that explained why she'd run each time they'd kissed. *Maybe the ex-boyfriend was only an excuse? Maybe she found him repulsive?*

He was certainly empty enough inside to repel most people. Though the way Chloe had kissed Ethan back made him think otherwise.

"Hey," he greeted. "Couldn't sleep?"

She shook her head and continued into the room. "You?"

He shook his head, too. "Not with the way Owen snores."

Chloe grinned. "Margot, too."

Ethan snorted a laugh. "They're perfect for each other."

Just then Ethan's stomach growled loudly.

Chloe looked at him quizzically. "Are you hungry?"

"I could go for some hot cocoa," he added, loving the way her cheeks flushed even in the dark.

It was difficult for him not to be flirtatious with her. He wasn't usually this forward but she just evoked a part of him that he wasn't aware he had. Normally, he left the cheesy pickup lines to his player of a brother. But with Chloe it was like the words that came out of Ethan's mouth developed somewhere other than his brain and he was unable to stop them from falling out of his mouth. Not that he minded. Because after the blush she smiled at him. *And that smile . . .*

Chloe, there's not a lot I wouldn't do to see that smile.

19

Chloe

CHLOE TRIED to get her heartbeat to slow down. She couldn't believe she'd run into Ethan two nights in a row. *Was he some sort of insomniac or had he been waiting for her?*

Chloe didn't know which answer she preferred. She had to admit when she woke up her first thoughts had been of him.

Of course they had. She'd fallen asleep thinking of his kiss and when she woke up at nearly midnight she knew she'd never fall back asleep with Margot's snoring. But ever the optimist, Chloe decided to make the most of her time and write in her journal. When that didn't help she finally decided on a cup of hot cocoa.

As she dressed in her pink, fuzzy robe, she wondered, maybe even hoped, she'd run into Ethan in the hall again. It almost made her look for a cuter alternative to her unflattering bathrobe. But in the end, comfort won out and she bundled up to head downstairs with her book, leaving Darcy snoring away with Margot.

After making it down the hallway and the stairs without running into Ethan, Chloe had thought she was safe. So when she saw someone move on the couch she nearly had a heart attack. She tried to tell herself that was why her heart was pounding in her chest. But clearly, Ethan's handsome face illuminated by the firelight didn't help the matter.

She needed to distance herself from him until she knew what she wanted. She didn't want to keep confusing him. Chloe kept her mind busy while she sorted through her hot cocoa stash, selecting a peppermint mocha mix to try. Tonight she managed to find a moderately tame Christmas mug. It was red with a candy cane striped handle and the words, *Merry Christmas,* printed in white. *At least it was store-bought.*

Chloe poured Ethan's hot cocoa into the mild holiday mug, saving the hand-painted penguin one for herself. She added some extra mini marshmallows, whipped cream and drizzled chocolate syrup on top of her concoction. Satisfied with her cocoa, she picked up both mugs and headed toward the living room, but she didn't get far. Ethan was leaning against the doorframe watching her. His eyes held a keen curiosity that made her skin warm.

A few months ago she would've given anything to have Brady look at her like that. Now Chloe wasn't sure if anyone's smoldering stare could compete with Ethan's.

It was funny how quickly things could change. Two days ago she'd never heard of Ethan Hall. But he'd quickly become the center of her universe—despite how hard she was fighting to deny it.

Chloe forced herself to walk confidently toward him. She handed him the mug, her blood sizzling the moment their fingers touched.

“Thanks,” he murmured.

"You're welcome," she replied, making her feet continue to carry her away from him. Half of her wanted to just go back upstairs and hide in her bedroom but if she did that now she'd be doing it the rest of winter break and Chloe refused to be uncomfortable in her own home.

Plus, who was she kidding? She would do nothing but think about Ethan if she went upstairs now.

Chloe could feel his eyes on her while she moved about the living room, turning the fireplace up and collecting her favorite blanket. One of the three Christmas trees in the living room had forced her favorite reading chair into the foyer, so Chloe was faced with only the worn leather couch or tiny plaid loveseat. She chose the couch. It faced the fireplace and at least it was large enough to share if Ethan decided to join her.

He did.

At first he settled on the arm of the couch, sipping from his mug. "This is even better than last night's cocoa," he said.

"Wait till you try the cinnamon horchata," she said. "That one's my favorite."

"Is that an invitation?"

Chloe could feel the air in the room change when Ethan spoke. *Was he flirting with her?*

Luckily when she looked at him she could see the amusement in his teasing smirk.

"So," he said. "Pine trees and hot cocoa, huh? That's what does it for you?"

She knew he was poking fun at her so she decided to go with it, holding up her book. "And don't forget cheesy romance novels."

He laughed.

The sound was thrilling.

"I like you better at night," Ethan added.

Chloe almost choked on her cocoa. "Is that supposed to be a compliment?"

He shrugged. "Maybe just an observation."

"Why do you like me better at night?"

"You talk more freely." He slid onto the couch. "And sometimes you kiss me."

Chloe laughed nervously, deciding to keep the teasing tone of their conversation, because she currently liked Ethan better at night, too. *At least he wasn't stabbing his chili and stomping away from her.* "I kiss you during the day, too," she teased, surprised by her boldness.

He shook his head. "No, I'm the one who kissed you today, Chloe."

She swallowed hard. *Okay, so maybe she wasn't as bold as she thought.* She couldn't casually flirt with him. Not when he said her name like that. It made her heart go haywire. She swallowed again. "Ethan . . ."

He interrupted her. "I know you have a boyfriend you're trying to get over."

"An ex-boyfriend," she corrected.

"Is that why you kissed me last night? To see if you're over him?"

Chloe squirmed under his gaze. She didn't know how to answer that question, because she didn't really know the answer herself. She kissed Ethan because she'd wanted to—because the increasing attraction between them was becoming impossible to resist. And if she wasn't careful, she was pretty sure she might kiss him again. "I shouldn't have kissed you, Ethan. I'm sorry."

His lopsided frown evened out. "I'm not."

An electric silence settled between them.

Ethan was the first to break it. "Can I ask you something?"

"Depends what it is."

"Why did you break up with your boyfriend?"

"Why do you want to know?"

"Because maybe if you think about all the reasons you don't want to be with him it'll help you get over him."

Chloe shook her head. "I don't think that'll work."

"Why not?"

"Because he broke up with me."

Ethan laughed. "Poor bastard."

"Poor bastard!" Chloe huffed. "What about me? I'm the one who got dumped."

"Yes, but you're gorgeous and enigmatic. Guys will be beating down the door to date you for the rest of your life. But this ex-boyfriend of yours is obviously a moron, and stupid isn't something he's likely to outgrow. Plus, if he does wise up he's just going to realize how bad he screwed up by letting a girl like you slip away. So ya see, the poor bastard can't win."

Chloe couldn't help but laugh. She'd never heard rejection described so eloquently. "Well, when you put it that way . . ." She laughed again, but then something Ethan said clicked. *Was that why Brady had come back? Had he realized he screwed up? Was he really trying to get her back?*

"What?" Ethan asked.

"Nothing, it's just something you said about my ex."

"He's the one who came looking for you at the lodge today, isn't he?"

Chloe nodded.

Ethan huffed a laugh. "Maybe he's not such a moron."

Chloe stared at Ethan trying to decipher his comment as he sipped his hot cocoa. She always felt there was so much meaning between his words. *Did he ever just say what he was thinking?*

It was maddening.

"It's my turn to ask you a question."

Ethan slid onto the couch, making himself comfortable. "Shoot."

"Why are you and your brother so different?"

Ethan smirked. "Picked up on that, did ya?"

"It's pretty easy to notice."

"You'd be surprised," he said. "Some people just see what they want to see. And when you're a carbon copy of someone else, your individuality can get overlooked."

"I know what you mean," Chloe said, thinking of how she always felt like the duller version of Margot.

"Is that why you try so hard to be nothing like your sister?" Ethan asked.

Chloe let her eyes meet Ethan's, surprised how well he read her. She wasn't ready to answer that question yet. "You still haven't answered my question," she teased.

But when she thought about what Ethan asked the answer surprised Chloe. She *did* try to be different from Margot. *Was that why she dressed drab and focused on books rather than herself?*

"Owen spent more time with our father than I did," Ethan said, drawing Chloe back to their conversation.

"Why?"

"He wasn't a pleasant man. Our parents separated because of it and that's about the time I stopped trying to get him to like me." He shrugged. "I figured if my mother wasn't successful then I'd never be."

He thought his father hated him?

Chloe didn't know what to do with that. "Oh," she said, softly. "Did they get divorced?"

"Eventually. It's my turn to ask a question."

"Okay."

"Tell me about your ex-boyfriend."

Chloe rolled her eyes. "Why are you so interested in him?"

"Because he seems to be the only thing standing between me and your lips."

Chloe felt heat wash her from head-to-toe. She swallowed thickly trying to slow her racing heart. "His name's Brady Jones. He lives next door."

Ethan groaned and let his head fall back against the couch. He brought his hand to his heart in a stabbing motion and sighed.

Chloe furrowed her brow. "What?"

"You didn't tell me I was competing with the boy next door."

"Competing?"

Ethan sat up, his crooked smirk back in place. "I thought I was being fairly obvious, Chloe. I like you. And despite your warnings, I can't stop thinking about kissing you."

"Oh," she said again.

He laughed. "You're not real good for my ego, Chloe."

"Sorry."

He shrugged. "Let's go back to our questions. I think it's your turn."

"Okay," she said. "Why aren't you in bed?"

"I told you, I couldn't sleep."

"But why?"

"Partly because of you, partly because of Owen's snoring and partly because it's Christmas Eve."

Chloe decided to skip over the first part of his answer. She wasn't ready to address the fact that he'd been thinking about her tonight, too. "You're a big Christmas Eve fan?"

"Not exactly."

She sighed. "Your answers always leave me with more questions."

"Maybe you should ask better questions. My turn. What's your favorite Christmas memory?"

She thought back, but all her memories muddled into one endless loop. It was hard when Christmas lasted all year in her house. "Honestly, they're all good. But I think my favorite Christmas was the year the pond froze and we all went ice skating on Christmas morning."

Ethan smiled. "How old were you?"

Chloe thought back. "Probably nine or ten. I used to love to ice skate."

Ethan's smirk grew.

"What?"

"I'm just imagining nine-year-old Chloe. You must've been a tornado of hair on ice," he teased tugging on a strand of hair sticking out from her messy topknot.

"Hey!" she swatted at his hand playfully. "I clean up when I try."

"I like that you don't try."

When Ethan looked at her it felt like all the air in the room had been vacuumed out. Chloe needed to keep him talking, otherwise she knew her lips would find a way to his. Before she could think of another question, Ethan asked one.

"So, ice skating, huh? Do you still do it?"

"No. It's been years since. The pond rarely freezes enough anymore and I don't even have a pair of skates that fit."

"Why not?"

She shrugged. "I don't know. I guess I just outgrew it." Chloe was noticing that was a theme lately. She'd outgrown her love of her family business, she'd outgrown her small town, she'd outgrown her skates, maybe she'd even outgrown Brady. Because for the life of her she couldn't remember a single thing about him that she liked better than every part of Ethan.

She pulled her blushing thoughts back to their conversation about skating. "I miss it," she said quietly. "My grandpa used to tell me he was going to take me skating at Rockefeller Center."

"Did he?"

She shook her head as sadness filled her heart. "He didn't get the chance."

"What happened?"

Chloe's eyes met Ethan's and she was grateful she didn't have to say the words. She recognized the understanding in his calm green eyes. She forced a smile. "Maybe some day I'll get to." Wanting to change the subject she asked Ethan another question. "What's your favorite Christmas memory?"

He shrugged. "Probably this."

"This? Sitting on a couch with a stranger? And it's not even Christmas."

"You're hardly a stranger, Chloe."

The way he said her name made her blood sizzle. Never had her name sounded so sexy. Chloe put her mug of cocoa on the coffee table. It was making her too hot. And so was the damn robe she was wearing. She untied the belt and shrugged out of it, laying it over the back of the couch.

Ethan watched her movements with interest.

"You know, you still haven't answered my question," she said as she got comfortable.

"Which one?"

"What's so special about Christmas Eve?"

Ethan's expression hardened and he took a sip of his cocoa.

Ethan

If Owen were here he'd be changing the subject right about now. He never wanted to talk about this. *But what did it matter if he told Chloe?* It's not like Ethan would be hurting his chances with her. She was hung up on her ex and in all likelihood Ethan would never see her again after he went back to Manhattan. Maybe saying the truth out loud would help him heal. *God knew nothing else had.*

Ethan pondered how to answer. Owen would be pissed, but it wasn't Ethan's fault that his brother hadn't told Margot all the messy details of their family. Owen should've thought of that before he brought Ethan here and intertwined their lives.

Besides, Margot would find out eventually if Owen was as serious about her as he said.

He set his mug of hot cocoa down on the coffee table and rested his elbows on his knees. "The thing about Christmas Eve is that it's the day Victoria Townsend died." He took a breath. "She was my mother."

The crackling of logs in the fireplace was the only sound in the room. Ethan focused on the dancing yellow-orange flames, watching the glowing embers pulse with life. The warmth coming from the hearth comforted him but it did little to dull the chill of his words.

He couldn't remember the last time he'd said her name out loud and he hated that. Before his mother died, her name had been everywhere. Her initials monogramed on pillows, purses, towels, and such. And it was always in the newspaper. 'New York Heiress donates millions' and other such headlines were synonymous with her name. Ethan was always so proud to call her his mother.

She had come from an extremely wealthy family—old money, born and bred in New York's high society. His father, however, had no money of his own before marrying Victoria. And if it were up to Alexander Hall, Ethan and Owen would've been left penniless and on the street the moment she died. Thankfully, Ethan's grandmother had stepped in to see that didn't happen. But it wasn't long before she left them, too. In the end, none of them had really been Ethan's to lose anyway.

He hadn't realized Chloe had moved closer until he felt her hand slip into his.

"I'm sorry," she said, softly.

He nodded, chewing hard on his bottom lip to keep his emotions in check.

"When did she pass away?" Chloe asked.

"Six years ago today."

"What happened to her?"

"Cancer."

Chloe squeezed his hand. "We don't have to talk about it."

"No," he said quickly, his eyes suddenly finding hers.

He was surprised to see something other than pity there. That wasn't what he craved. He craved understanding, compassion, connection. And he saw each of those emotions in Chloe's bright eyes. They glowed like liquid amber in the firelight and Ethan wanted to drown in them.

He wanted to dive in and bathe in Chloe's warmth and beauty, leaving his sorrow behind. He wanted to let her kiss away all the grief that refused to ever fully let go of him. But more than that, he wanted to feel he was allowed to miss his mother. Because he did—*even after everything she kept from him.*

20

Chloe

CHLOE SAT SILENTLY next to Ethan, keeping a gentle pressure on his hand to let him know she was there. She didn't know what to say. It was clear Ethan was struggling with his emotions. *How could he not be?*

She couldn't imagine how she would ever deal with losing either of her parents, especially at such a young age. Sure, she didn't *love* having to spend all her free time working in the family business, but she loved her family. She loved how she always knew they were there for her and how she could talk to them when she needed to. It was something she suddenly realized she'd taken for granted.

Memories of some of her favorite times with her parents began to flash through Chloe's mind. Ice fishing with her father, baking Christmas cookies and pies with her mother, riding on her father's shoulders when they walked through the rows of Christmas trees, her mother teaching her to cook and play piano and drive and everything else in between. She'd miss it all. Even the way they ridiculously broke into dance anytime a song they loved came on the radio. Her family was her world.

But one day they would be gone.

An overwhelming sadness gripped Chloe as she thought about what it would be like if she'd lost out on even a single moment she'd had with them. Those moments would have to be enough to sustain her one day. The thought left a hole in her heart. Ethan's mother was already gone. He wouldn't have very many memories to carry with him.

"Would you tell me about her?" Chloe finally asked.

Ethan looked surprised, his green eyes bright in the firelight. "My mother?"

"Yes."

"Do you really want to know?"

"I do."

Ethan sat back on the couch, watching the fire with a strange smile on his face. It was almost a full one—*almost*. But Chloe couldn't help noticing that the slightest hint of frown remained. Maybe the weight of the grief he carried wouldn't let him smile with his whole heart. She could understand that.

"No one's asked me to talk about her in so long I don't even know where to start."

"How old was she?"

Ethan looked at her again, pain in his eyes. "Forty-one."

Chloe's heart dropped. *Her mother was forty-one.* She couldn't imagine losing her now. She still seemed so young and vibrant. "You said she had cancer?"

"Yes. Lung cancer." He shook his head. "You know she never even smoked a cigarette once." His knuckles tightened around the mug. "It should've been him."

"Who?" Chloe asked.

"My so-called father. He *still* smokes. If the world was fair he would've been the one to get lung cancer."

Chloe heard the unmistakable hurt in Ethan's voice. His words were harsh and he most likely didn't mean them, but she couldn't hold it against him. She had no idea how she would react if she were in Ethan's shoes. She imagined grief of this magnitude could freeze even the warmest of hearts.

"So your father is still alive?" Chloe asked.

Ethan huffed a laugh. "Alive and well. He's actually on an Alaskan cruise with his new family right now. They go every year."

Chloe's mouth fell open. "And you and Owen aren't invited?"

"No."

Chloe watched the muscles in Ethan's jaw feather with anger. She didn't want to push him, so she sat quietly next to him, still holding his cold hand.

"He got remarried a few months after my mother died. He has two new children with his new wife. I've never met them."

"You've never met your half siblings?"

Ethan slowly shook his head. "They're not my half anything." He took the saddest breath she'd ever heard before continuing. "After my mother died we found out we were adopted. My father told us. He tried to have us cut out of the will when he found out my mother left all of her wealth to us. He told us he'd never even wanted us and that it was our mother's idea to adopt us. So not only did we lose our mother that Christmas, but the only family we'd ever known."

"Ethan . . ." Chloe felt the way Ethan began to tremble and she took the mug from him so she could hold both of his hands, squeezing them in hers. She felt tears of sympathy pressing at her eyes when she took in the anguish on Ethan's face. The firelight made his grief seem etched in stone. "That's . . . I don't even know what to say."

He tried to laugh but it was a bitter, strangled sound. "Neither did I."

"Did your father really disown you?"

"He tried, but my grandmother stepped in. She made sure my mother's wishes were carried out."

A tiny bit of comfort filled Chloe momentarily. *At least Ethan and Owen hadn't been totally alone.* "She sounds like a good person."

"She was," Ethan replied.

Was? Chloe was afraid to ask.

"My grandmother passed away four years ago. Owen was eighteen so I filed for emancipation so we could both be granted access to our inheritance."

Inheritance? Emancipation? Ethan's life sounded so foreign to Chloe that she found the bond growing between them strange, but it was there nonetheless. She hated that his life had been full of so much pain and loss, while hers had been mostly carefree.

But maybe that was what bonded them?

She was strong where he was weak. She was stable where he was unsteady. She was whole where he was broken. Maybe she was what he needed. The connection she felt to him was undeniable and now that he had opened up to her, she understood why. She'd always loved healing people—and she'd never met someone who needed to be healed more than Ethan Hall.

"I'm so sorry, Ethan. I had no idea."

"How could you? It's not like anyone in my family ever talks about it."

"Why not?"

He shrugged. "It's like everyone just wants to get over it and move on."

Chloe's heart cracked wide open. "Ethan, I know I don't really know you that well, but what happened to you and your brother . . . that's not something you should ever be expected to get over."

"I know," he said sadly. "I try not to dwell on it. Things could be worse. I have a good life. And I have Owen. But sometimes it's just hard. Especially around Christmas."

"I'm sorry," she said again. "I didn't mean to make things worse."

He gave her a tight smile. "You didn't. Actually, it's kind of nice to talk about this."

Chloe squeezed Ethan's hands. "I can listen if you want to talk more," she offered.

A small kernel of hope blossomed in Ethan's green eyes. "You don't mind?"

"Not at all." Chloe scooted closer to him on the couch, pulling her favorite fuzzy plaid blanket between them.

Ethan pulled the corner of it over his legs and smiled. "I think you would've liked her. I know the rest of your family would have."

"Why's that?"

"My mother was crazy about Christmas, too."

Chloe laughed. "Then she'd probably fit in here better than I do."

Ethan offered her a half smile. "I think you fit in better than you think."

Chloe pulled the blanket up higher. "Tell me something else. What was her favorite thing about Christmas?"

Ethan's face lit up. "Christmas movies. Owen loves them, too."

"Just your mom and Owen?" she teased.

"I'm afraid I like them, too. Or I used to. That's actually why I came down here tonight. I was going to watch, *Miracle on 34th Street*. It was her favorite movie. We used to watch it with her every Christmas Eve."

"I've never seen that one," Chloe admitted.

Ethan's eyebrows shot up. “You've never seen *Miracle on 34th Street*?”

“No. Is it really that good?”

“Wow, I can't believe I kissed a girl with such abysmal taste in movies.” Ethan reached for his laptop. “We’re going to have to rectify this immediately.” He started to queue up the movie. “How is it possible that you don't have every Christmas movie memorized living in this house?”

Chloe rolled her eyes. “That's the problem. Christmas is year-round here. Sometimes I need a break. I usually read whenever my parents put on a movie.”

“Is that where the cheesy romance novels come in?” he teased.

“Hey, until you read one you can’t knock it.”

“Are you forgetting I’ve read *Pride and Prejudice*? I know all about cheesy romance.”

“I haven’t forgotten. But Jane Austen is hardly cheesy.”

“Okay I'll make you a deal. For every Christmas movie you watch with me I'll read one of your books.”

Chloe arched her eyebrow. “Seriously?”

“Why not? I need a break from all the memories Christmas movies inspire and you need a break from unrealistic romance.”

“Unrealistic romance?”

Ethan gave her an amused look. “Don’t tell me you think real life can be wrapped up into happily ever afters?”

“I didn’t say that.”

“I’m just saying if you read more realist novels maybe you wouldn’t get your heart broken.”

Chloe cut her eyes at Ethan. “Who said Brady broke my heart?”

He shrugged. “I just figured if you're still hung up on him . . . But don't listen to me. I've never had a girlfriend.”

“I find that hard to believe.”

"Why?"

"Have you looked in the mirror?"

Ethan

Ethan frowned. He hated that Chloe said that. His looks were his least favorite thing about himself. *How could he like the way he looked when it wasn't original?*

He was just a younger, sadder version of Owen. And if Chloe only liked Ethan for his looks then maybe she wasn't the girl he thought she was. Although, she didn't seem able to recognize her own simple beauty, so Ethan decided to let the comment go.

"Looks aren't everything," he said, pressing play on the movie.

The theme song came on and his heart filled with bittersweet nostalgia. A tear slid down his cheek and he felt Chloe watching him. After he quickly wiped his eyes, Chloe did something unexpected. She scooted closer on the couch and slipped her hand into his, letting it rest on his lap as her head settled against his shoulder.

That simple gesture made him feel so much less alone that he could've cried for the sheer joy of it. He'd never imagined following Owen on this strange holiday excursion would have ever brought him any comfort or joy, but then again Ethan had never imagined meeting someone like Chloe.

Chloe

Chloe held onto Ethan's hand like a lifeline as they watched the sappy Christmas movie. She couldn't stop thinking about all that he'd been through. Her heart broke for him and she wished there was more she could do, but she was glad she could at least be there for him now. From the way he squeezed her hand during the sentimental parts of the movie it was obvious he needed someone to share this with.

Knowing what Ethan had been through made Chloe contemplate her own family and how terrible it would be if she lost them. Chloe felt like a total ingrate having complained about working at her family's business in front of Ethan. He'd probably do anything to be part of a family like hers, no matter how crazy they were about Christmas.

It certainly put things in perspective. Maybe this was why Margot had brought the Hall brothers to their home for Christmas. They were both in some need of healing, and nothing could heal like the magic of the holidays at Everett's.

21

Chloe

Dawn light bled in through the heavy wool curtains, the red and white Tartan pattern giving everything a rustic glow. At first Chloe forgot where she was, but as she awoke to the warmth of the muscled body next to hers, her mind snapped back into focus.

She was nestled beneath a blanket on her living room couch, her body curled alongside Ethan's in a way that suggested they'd been much more intimate than they had. Her head rested on his chest, his arm draped over her back. For a moment she couldn't tear herself away. She drank in his delicious boy smell and sank into the comfortable rise and fall of his chest beneath her cheek.

The feeling of contentment that washed over Chloe evaporated as soon as she heard the stairs creak. Her head snapped up, the sudden movement jerking Ethan awake.

“What's wrong?” he asked.

“We fell asleep,” she whisper-hissed as she untangled herself from him.

Ethan sat up and stretched, his dark hair sticking out every which way. Sleep still clung to his eyes. His drowsiness only made him more adorable to Chloe but she couldn't think about that now. Any second her parents would be in the living room and she needed to come up with a good excuse for why she was sleeping on the couch with a half-dressed boy.

They hadn't done anything wrong but it certainly didn't look that way with Ethan’s shirt on the floor and Chloe pulling on her bathrobe. They had the fire turned up so high during the movie that they'd had to shed some of their layers. Then they must've fallen asleep. The last thing Chloe remembered was holding Ethan's hand . . . *and his mother!*

Everything he’d shared with her came crashing back, making Chloe halt her frantic hustling as Ethan’s heartbreaking story filled her with a heaviness she knew would never leave. *How did he carry that around every day?*

She wanted to say something to him, tell him she was glad he’d opened up to her and that she’d be there for him, but the sound of a throat clearing made her pause.

Margot’s cheery voice greeted them. “Well, good morning. What's going on here?”

“Nothing,” Chloe said, snatching Ethan’s shirt from the floor and handing it to him.

He gave her a wry smile and pulled the shirt on. It only made his sleep stiff hair wilder and somehow sexier.

Owen stopped short when he came into the living room behind Margot. “Bro, nice bed head!”

“Did you guys sleep out here?” Margot asked, suspicion heavy in her voice. “Together?”

“We were just watching a movie,” Chloe said, defensively.

Owen stiffened as his eyes met Ethan’s. Chloe noticed the

look they shared. It was the same one from the dinner table the first night. *Owen knew exactly what movie they'd been watching.*

So why hadn't he been there watching it alongside his brother?

A fierce protectiveness flared up in Chloe. Up until that moment she thought she liked Owen. He seemed like the kinder, more affectionate brother, but now that Chloe understood the situation she wasn't so sure. *How could Owen let his brother suffer alone?*

There was no way he didn't know what Ethan was going through. They were brothers for God's sake! If they were anything like Chloe and Margot they'd have to feel each other's pain. Chloe knew when Margot was upset just by walking into a room.

Chloe had always known she and her sister had a close relationship. She often thought of them like bookends—*one virtually useless without the other.*

That's partly why the past few months had been so difficult for Chloe. Without her sister's support she felt herself slipping into uncertainty. *So how could Owen not know his brother needed him? And what about Owen? Surely the holidays were taking a toll on him as well?*

Chloe watched Margot who was watching the silent exchange between the brothers. Chloe suddenly wondered just how much Margot knew about her boyfriend's past.

Chloe glanced at the clock. It wasn't even seven. "Why are you up so early?"

"Snowmobiling, remember?"

"Oh. Right." *She'd completely forgot.*

"I'm going to go put the coffee on," Margot said, giving Chloe a wary look as she walked by.

"Snowmobiling?" Ethan asked.

"Yeah, Brady invited us," Owen added as he followed Margot into the kitchen, leaving Ethan with his own guarded glance.

When Chloe looked back at Ethan, he was staring at her. The intensity of his gaze made her self-conscious. She probably looked awful after a night on the couch, not to mention her breath didn't smell like roses. She took a step back but Ethan didn't seem to understand her hesitation. He reached for her, tucking a loose strand of hair behind her ear. It had fallen out of her bun and was cascading down her back like a static-y, brown waterfall.

Chloe had never really liked wearing her hair down. She didn't take the time necessary to tame her unruly waves. But the way Ethan ran his fingers over the loose strands still in his hand made it seem like he was holding threads of magic.

"Chloe," he said, his voice still rough with sleep. "Last night . . ." he ran his hand down her arm, leaving shivers in its wake until he linked his fingers with hers. "Thank you."

Ethan rubbed his thumb ever so slightly over the back of Chloe's hand erasing the words she'd been about to say. She couldn't think. Not with the feel of his hand on hers or the warmth in his words. She'd never known two little words could hold so much hope, but she felt it blossom in her chest. *'Thank you.'* She wanted to say it back to him. She wanted to say *'Thank you for sharing your heart with me. I'll protect it. I promise.'*

But before she could say anything the doorbell rang and Darcy came bolting down the stairs like a ferocious bolt of lightning.

Brady! Dammit! He knew better than to ring the obnoxious, *Jingle Bells*, doorbell.

"Coming!" Chloe called trying to grab Darcy, but Brady opened the door before she could catch the dog.

Brady knew better than to do that, too. He'd been to Chloe's house a million times. He knew not to open the door until the furry Houdini was leashed. In a flash, Darcy was past Brady, bounding through the snow.

"Grab him!" Chloe shouted.

. . .

BRADY

"OH NO!" Margot yelled, running to the door. "Darcy got out?"

"What's the problem?" Owen was asking.

"He'll run onto the road," Chloe yelled tugging her boots on over her pajama pants. "Why did you open the door?" she muttered at Brady.

"I thought you said, 'come in'."

"I said, '*coming*'!"

"Oh," Brady frowned. "Well, don't worry. I'll get him, Clo."

"He won't come to you," she grumbled reaching for her coat.

"Trust me," he said, pulling the leash from her hands. "I've got this." Then he planted a kiss on top of her wild hair and jogged back out the open door.

Brady patted his pocket, making sure the bacon was still there. It was his secret weapon. His plan to win Chloe back was working perfectly. Brady knew she would be super impressed if he caught Darcy. That dog meant the world to her and they'd all spent many a night chasing the crazy furball through the woods. He might be tiny but he ran like he was powered by rocket fuel. No one had ever been able to catch him once he escaped. He ran until he had his fill and then he only came to Chloe. But Brady knew Darcy would do anything for bacon.

He smiled to himself as he followed the little dog's tracks. "Darcy," he called. "Come here, buddy. I've got something for you."

In no time he'd return a hero and Chloe would be eating out of the palm of his hand, just like Darcy would be any minute.

22

Ethan

ETHAN WATCHED Brady return victorious with the tiny Yorkie in his arms. The dog was furiously licking his fingers and anger began to unfurl in Ethan's stomach. He didn't like this guy one bit. And not just because he was Chloe's ex.

Okay, that had a lot to do with it, but something seemed shady about Brady.

Ethan had been in college long enough to be able to spot a guy on his game. And this guy was tipping the douchebag meter off the charts.

Brady waltzed into the house, placing the dog into Chloe's waiting arms, making sure he got in on all the hugging, too. "I told you I'd get him," he said with a cocky grin.

"Brady to the rescue!" Margot exclaimed, snuggling the little dog.

“Thank you,” Chloe said, gazing up at Brady with adoration.

“Anything for you, Clo.”

Ethan almost gagged aloud. Instead he cracked his knuckles, the sudden urge to punch something seizing him again. *Tell me you can see through his BS, Chloe?*

“So, who's ready to go snowmobiling?” Brady asked.

“Sorry," Chloe said. "We got a bit of a late start. We haven't had breakfast yet."

"That's okay," Brady replied. "My mom packed breakfast for the four of us. I figured we could eat once we got up to Pine Ridge.”

BRADY

CHLOE'S EYES darted to Owen’s moody brother standing by the stairs. Brady had asked around about Ethan last night. He hadn't liked the way the older boy’s eyes never left Chloe when they were at the lodge. And he liked the way Ethan was looking at her now even less. The guy was a total buzzkill. It was like he didn't know how to smile.

But even with his stoic scowl, it was clear that he had it bad for Chloe. Brady couldn't blame him, but he didn't need any competition while he was trying to win her back.

Luckily, he’d noticed Ethan was into Chloe last night and planned ahead. There was only room for four on the two snowmobiles. *Sorry, Ethan. No room for broody fifth wheels.*

“There are five of us, Brady," Chloe said.

Brady played dumb. “Five? Oh, hey man,” he said, striding toward Ethan. “Did you want to come, too? I’m Brady by the way, Chloe’s boyfriend.”

Chloe cleared her throat and Brady pretended to be embarrassed. "Sorry. Old habit. I meant to say, I'm Chloe's best friend. It's nice to meet you."

Chloe

CHLOE RESISTED the urge to hold her breath as she waited for Ethan to shake Brady's hand. *This wasn't ideal—her ex-boyfriend meeting her new . . . her new what?*

Frustration overcame her. She hated that she and Ethan kept getting interrupted. Maybe if they had a minute to spend together without being disturbed she could figure out how she felt, but with her family and neighbors butting in Chloe couldn't catch her breath.

She sighed, already exhausted by this morning's hectic start. And if Ethan didn't shake Brady's hand, things were only going to get worse.

Relief swept through Chloe as Ethan finally extended his hand. She didn't miss the look of disapproval in Ethan's eyes though. *Those eyes.* They were so damn expressive. Chloe felt like she could read his thoughts just by looking at him. And right now he was thinking, *'the feeling's not mutual, Brady.'*

"I'm sorry, man," Brady was saying. "I didn't know you wanted to go. I only have two sleds. There's not room for all of us."

"We can take one of ours," Chloe said, interrupting whatever response Ethan had been about to give.

The last thing she wanted was for Ethan to feel left out. Besides, she really wanted him to come. If Owen had never been snowmobiling then Ethan probably hadn't either. It was really fun and Ethan needed joy in his life more than anyone. Plus, she couldn't help feeling a bit giddy about the idea of having Ethan's arms wrapped around her on a snowmobile.

"Does our snowmobile still run?" Margot asked.

"I'm sure it does," Chloe replied.

"But it's so old."

That was true. Her father bought new snowmobiles for the lodge every few years but they still had one from the nineties for their personal use. "You know Dad. I'm sure he keeps it tuned up."

Chloe was about to ask Margot if she would go check it out with her. Chloe really wanted to talk to her sister about the things Ethan had revealed last night, but a look around the room of burly boys made Chloe think better of leaving them alone. The way Ethan and Brady were scowling at each other didn't bode well. Instead, she grabbed Ethan's hand. "Come with me. I'll find you some warm clothes you can borrow."

23

Ethan

"You don't have to do this," Ethan said, standing next to Chloe as she tried revving the snowmobile.

"I want to," Chloe argued. "Now get on."

Ethan looked at the two sleek black snowmobiles Brady had brought. Owen and Margot were on one and a scowling Brady was on the other. They looked brand new, their engines purring as they revved them, while the ancient red snowmobile Chloe had dusted off smelled like a lawnmower and sounded like one, too.

Ethan looked back at Chloe who was sitting on the old sled, looking like a pro. "Are you sure you don't just want to go with them? I can stay here."

"I want to go with you," she said confidently.

Each word slammed into his heart with alarming precision.

Please mean that, Chloe. I don't think I can let go if I let you in any further.

After talking to her last night, Ethan had the best night of sleep since . . . well, since he could remember. She was like a drug, tranquilizing all the pain and trauma he carried around with him. When he let himself just be with her, he felt the closest to happy he'd ever been. And he knew climbing onto that snowmobile and wrapping his arms around her would be like climbing into a life raft. Either they would survive the storm that lived inside him or he'd drown them both.

Anxiety filled him as he glanced back over his shoulder to where the others were laughing and doing donuts in their fast new snowmobiles.

"Ethan," Chloe called.

When he looked back at her she was extending her hand and without hesitation he took it and climbed aboard.

Chloe grinned and wrapped his arms around her waist. "Hold on tight and don't let go unless I tell you to, okay?"

He took a deep breath and nodded.

Chloe, I don't think I could let go now if I wanted to.

Chloe

BY THE TIME they reached Pine Ridge, Chloe was certain the sound of Ethan's laughter was more than enough to keep her warm for an eternity. It was just one more piece of him she'd found irresistibly attractive. He was sparing with his smiles and even more so with his laughter, so when she got a rare laugh it created a pull in her chest that she was beginning to crave.

There were so many pieces to this boy who held onto her with a grip of steel, and she found she wanted to learn about each of them. The only hesitation chipping away at her joy was their timeline. Ethan wasn't hers. He was only here for a few days and if she let things go too far both of them would end up more broken than ever. And that was the last thing she wanted for him.

She shook the thought away and cranked the throttle. Ethan gripped her tighter, chasing away her fears.

THEY REACHED the peak much later than everyone else, but Chloe didn't mind. She kind of liked that their snowmobile was slower. It gave her and Ethan time to themselves. They hadn't really been able to talk. It was too hard to hear over the roar of the engine and the hiss of snow and trees that flew by in a blur. But still, it was nice to just be with him. Even in the quiet moments she spent with him, Chloe found herself liking him more and more.

When they finally climbed off their snowmobile, everyone was finishing the meal Brady had packed. Chloe noticed there was more than enough food for all of them. A tiny seed of anger settled in her stomach when she remembered how ready Brady had been to exclude Ethan from today's excursion.

It was true Brady didn't know what Ethan had been through, but then again that might not have changed his mind. It was one of the things Chloe liked least about Brady. He was usually so focused on himself that he didn't notice what others were going through. He certainly hadn't noticed that he'd destroyed her when he dumped her in front of everyone at school.

Chloe tried to push the memory away. She'd told him she'd forgiven him and she'd meant it. But that didn't instantly erase the pain that still lived in her heart. It seemed to grow worse in his presence, making Chloe wonder if it would ever go away.

Perhaps once someone you trust hurts you in a way you never could've fathomed, no amount of forgiveness can make you forget the pain.

She looked at Brady, searching him with new eyes. He'd apologized to her and she appreciated it, but it didn't change the fact that a part of her would never be the same. He'd broken her trust and though she was grateful to have him back in her life as a friend, she knew with sudden clarity that they could never be more again.

Strangely, that realization was freeing. And as she watched him chatting easily with Owen she saw Brady in a different light. He was attractive, yes. But beyond his physical appearance, she found herself wondering why she'd ever thought he was the be-all, end-all.

She and Brady had very little in common other than the location of their homes. He didn't have the depth she craved. Everything was at face value with Brady. At first, Chloe thought that was a good thing. It was nice to know what he was thinking at all times. But now as she watched him clearly excluding Ethan from the conversation he was having with Owen, she hated what she read on Brady's face —*supremacy*.

Chloe glanced at Ethan. He was so much different than Brady, and even Owen. It was harder for him to let people in. But then again, there was something special about that. Chloe liked that she'd had to earn enough trust to be privy to his thoughts and feelings.

Now, observing the way Ethan stood off to the side, watching everyone, waiting, she knew it wasn't because he was standoffish or had a superiority complex. Others might mistake it for that, but Chloe knew better. She understood what held him back. It was fear. He'd been cast out so many times that it left a permanent scar.

Unlike Brady, Ethan didn't know where he belonged in a group. It wasn't any wonder why. He was abandoned over and over by those who were supposed to be there for him—*his birth parents, his adoptive parents, possibly even Owen.*

Owen certainly wasn't showing any signs of the pain Ethan carried. Chloe couldn't help wondering why that was. There was so much more Chloe wanted to know about the brothers. But the apprehensive look in Ethan's eyes told her that right now it was more important to let him know why she invited him to come with her.

"Ethan, are you hungry?" she asked, walking around the snowmobile.

He nodded.

Chloe grabbed one of the foil-wrapped breakfast sandwiches and passed it to Ethan.

He unwrapped it. "Do you want half?"

"No thanks."

"She's a vegetarian," Brady added, butting into their conversation.

Ethan took a bite of his sandwich. "Well, good thing you brought her a ham and cheese sandwich then."

Brady looked livid. "I brought more than that, but you guys took so long getting here we ate the fruit I packed."

"It's okay," Chloe interjected. "I brought my own stuff," she said, pulling a granola bar and apple from her pocket.

Brady huffed and walked back over to his snowmobile muttering under his breath. When he was gone, Chloe relaxed a little. She was glad to see Ethan was contently eating his sandwich. She knew he had to be starving. All he'd had since lunch yesterday was the hot cocoa she'd made him last night.

Suddenly, her comment from dinner came rushing back to her. *'Didn't your mom ever make chili?'*

She groaned internally. She was such an idiot. *Way to bring up the fact that he didn't have a mother to cook him meals, Clo.*

His reaction made more sense now. Wanting desperately to make it up to him, Chloe patted the empty spot on the snowmobile next to her. She wanted to make sure he knew she was there for him.

It was Christmas Eve. Today couldn't be easy for him and it was important to Chloe that he knew he wasn't alone.

Ethan hesitantly moved toward her, but Brady returned from his sled and slid into the empty spot next to Chloe before Ethan got a chance.

"So," Brady said slinging a heavy arm around her neck. "Who wants to race to the ice fields?"

"Oh my God!" Margot exclaimed. "We haven't done that since we were kids. This place brings back memories. I need to come up here more often."

Brady looked slyly at Chloe. "We were up here not too long ago, remember, Clo?"

Chloe's cheeks heated. Of course she remembered. It was one of the first nights they'd spent together when they were dating. They'd taken Brady's quad up to the peak and watched the sunset. They hadn't seen much of it though since they were too busy exploring each other.

Embarrassment and shame mixed in her stomach making her lose her appetite. She didn't want to think about that night or all the other nights that she'd been stupid enough to give herself to a boy who'd so easily given her away when someone better came along. She desperately wanted to change the subject but for the life of her couldn't think of a thing to say.

It was silly. She knew no one else would get Brady's reference, but she still hated the fact that he'd brought it up. Whatever game he was playing, she didn't like it.

"So, what do ya say?" Brady pushed, looking directly at Ethan. "You up for a little friendly competition?"

Chloe shrugged out from under Brady's arm and walked over to Ethan, offering him some of her water. "Actually, I was thinking I'd show Ethan how to drive on the way back."

Ethan gave her a rare, almost-smile. "I'd like that."

"Good," she said softly, letting her hand linger on his when he passed the water canteen back.

"Nice. You show him the ropes and then we'll race," Brady added.

"I don't really feel like racing," Chloe said.

"Fine, I'd rather race the guys anyway," Brady argued. "You and Margot can time us. What do ya think?" he asked looking back at Margot and Owen. "Margot!" Brady shouted.

Margot pulled her lips away from Owen's, looking startled. "What?"

Brady growled. "You guys are no fun."

Margot giggled, placing a peck on Owen's lips. "I'm having lots of fun," she said. "How 'bout you, babe?"

Chloe loved her sister so much in that moment. Sometimes she wished she could be as unapologetic as Margot. The girl went after what she wanted and owned it. *Speaking of what she wanted*... Chloe found her eyes wandering to Ethan's lips.

"Do you want to take a walk?" she asked.

"Sure."

24

Ethan

THE ICE GLISTENED like dangling spires of glass on the bare tree limbs they passed under. Everywhere Ethan looked the world was white and glittering with snow. Yesterday had been a record snowfall for the area.

Ethan found he enjoyed being the first to walk over the freshly fallen snow. It was like he was blazing his own path, heading in a direction of his own making—one without expectations or a past. Sometimes he wished his life could be that way.

He breathed the frigid air in deeply, trying to hold onto this perfect moment. He liked being out in the quiet, snowy world with Chloe. "It's beautiful out here," he said.

"It is."

They walked a little way more before he stopped and turned to face her. "So what did you want to talk about?"

Her gorgeous eyes widened, allowing him to see their full brilliance. “How did you know I wanted to talk?”

Ethan grinned. “You’re pretty easy to read.”

She pouted. “My mom always says she never knows what’s on my mind.”

He huffed a laugh. “I find that hard to believe.”

“Why?”

“Your eyes are like two windows right into your thoughts.”

Chloe crossed her arms. “Okay, smart guy. What am I thinking right now?”

Ethan took his time, enjoying being able to study her unabashed. “You’re thinking that I’m the most interesting guy you’ve ever met, you’re a little bit hungry still since Brady ate your breakfast, and you’re wondering what you ever saw in a douche-nozzle like him in the first place.”

Chloe laughed out loud.

“Spot on?” he teased.

“Surprisingly, some of that is pretty accurate.”

Ethan arched an eyebrow, impressed that she was admitting he’d pegged her. “Which parts?”

“If you can read me so easily, shouldn’t you be telling me?”

Ethan studied her again, not liking what he saw. “You’re worried about me.”

He saw confirmation in Chloe’s eyes. “I am,” she said, quietly.

Ethan didn’t reply.

“You can really tell what I’m thinking just from looking at my eyes?”

He nodded, growing uncomfortable with where this conversation was heading. He’d been hoping to keep things light after last night had been so serious. Ethan shoved his hands into his pockets and started walking again. Chloe caught up with him and pulled him to a stop.

“I *am* worried about you,” she said. “Last night . . .”

"I'm sorry," he interrupted. "Last night was a little much. I don't usually get like that. It's just the holidays . . ." He sighed. "They're never easy."

"Ethan, I don't want you to apologize for last night. I wanted to tell you that I'm really glad you opened up to me."

Her hand tentatively reached for his.

He let her take it.

"I can't imagine it's easy to deal with your emotions this time of year and I just wanted you to know that I'm here for you if you need someone to talk to . . . or not talk to," she added.

It was a struggle to speak around the lump in his throat. "Thank you," Ethan said, finding himself wishing there was a better way to express his gratitude. This was the second time he'd found himself at a loss for words around Chloe. Saying 'thank you' just wasn't enough to convey what her compassion meant to him.

She smiled at him and squeezed his hand. "Anytime."

He looked longingly at her lips. *You're making it hard not to fall for you, Chloe.*

Ethan wanted to pull her into his arms and kiss her right there beneath the frosted pines. But he knew if he kissed her again it would be all over. He'd already let her in more than he intended. Last night had been a surprise to him. He hadn't planned to tell Chloe everything but once he had he couldn't believe how much better he felt. He needed to stop bottling up his emotions and Chloe made it easy for him. Ethan looked at her trying to school his features. *What are you doing to me, Chloe?*

He enjoyed being with her and talking to her. He wanted to let her in all the way—*but should he?*

Ethan had come to Pine Island to salvage the little family he had left this Christmas, not tear apart another one, which was surely what would happen if he continued to pursue his feelings for Chloe.

So as usual, Ethan forced his emotions back down and said nothing.

Chloe

CHLOE WALKED side-by-side with Ethan further into the woods. For a while she was quiet, but the silence between them was changing. She could feel him withdrawing and she hated it. After everything he'd shared with her last night and the warmth she'd seen in him this morning she couldn't let it go. Not when she knew he was hurting and she could do something about it.

"Can I ask you something?" she asked, tentatively.

"If you'd like."

"Why do you hate chili?"

He stopped walking and looked at her quizzically with his sad eyes. "I don't hate chili."

"But at dinner last night . . ."

"That was an overreaction," he replied, his jaw twitching with tension.

"I didn't mean to upset you," she said, recalling her comment. "I mean, by asking why your mom didn't make chili for you. I just didn't know you'd lost her."

A sad expression took over Ethan's entire face. It twisted a knife in Chloe's heart to see him like that. *Maybe she was wrong. Maybe she was making things worse.*

"You didn't upset me," he said slowly. "I was already upset."

"Why?"

Ethan sighed and rubbed a hand across his jaw. "I lied. I have had chili before. Once. With my mother."

Chloe stayed quiet, waiting for him to continue.

"I was young. We were on a ski trip. She wasn't feeling well enough to ski so I stayed in the lodge with her. We ordered chili and watched a movie together. Just the two of us."

Chloe could tell he was working through his emotions.

"It's one of my favorite memories with her. And until last night, I hadn't let myself think of it in a very long time."

"It's okay to remember her," Chloe said, softly.

Ethan started to shake his head. "No. No, it's not. Because when I think of her I miss her and it hurts too much." He shook his head again. "I can't explain it. You wouldn't understand."

"I might," she said.

Ethan looked at her with so much hope in his sad green eyes that it nearly cut off her air supply. *Please,* she prayed, *please let me understand.* She desperately wanted to be what Ethan needed so she could ease his pain.

"Have you ever lost someone you loved, Chloe?"

She nodded. "My grandpa. He died a few years ago. It was pretty unexpected," she said, feeling that familiar ache that flooded her chest whenever she thought about him and how much emptier the world felt without his booming laughter.

Ethan put his hand over her heart. "That," he said. "That feeling. It sucks. And it's what consumes me every time I let myself think of her."

Chloe nodded. She *did* understand. "My grandpa had a heart attack. He passed away in his sleep. One day he was there and the next . . ." she trailed off. "I remember thinking that it wasn't real. Like any minute he'd walk in the door and fill the house with his laughter." She smiled. "He had the best laugh."

Ethan was studying her with those sharp green eyes that cut her to the core. When he looked at her like that it made it feel like someone ripped a hole in her chest, exposing her fragile heart to all the dangers of the world.

"How did you move past it?" he asked.

Chloe reached up and placed her hands on either side of his cheeks. "My grandpa was ninety. He had a good life. I can't compare losing him to you losing your mother. They're not the same. But what I can tell you is that when I do find myself thinking of him, I let the pain in."

He closed his eyes. "I can't."

"Why not?"

He began to tremble and it wasn't from the cold. "I'm not as strong as you, Chloe."

"You're stronger than you think," she whispered, kissing his cheek.

Ethan opened his eyes, his desperate stare stealing all the air in her lungs.

Ethan

ETHAN OPENED his eyes and stared desperately at Chloe as he felt the protective walls around his heart cracking and falling away. *You make me feel stronger than I am, Chloe. You make me feel everything. And you make me want to fight. You make me want to beat back the depression that wins nearly every daily battle. But you're not mine, Chloe. You'll leave me, too. It's not your fault. Everyone leaves…*

Ethan swallowed back all the words he didn't have the courage to say because he knew they wouldn't make a difference. The strength he was feeling only happened in Chloe's presence. With his fingers tightly clutching hers he felt like he could weather any storm. But that wouldn't last. Winter break would end and so would this feeling of hope Chloe filled him with. Like everyone else in his life, she wasn't really his.

All he truly had was Owen. But even he was slipping away, having found hope and strength in Margot.

Ethan took a shuddering breath. "I'm not strong, Chloe." *I'm a coward, because I'm too afraid to make you mine.*

. . .

Chloe

"YES, you are. And if you let your feelings in you'll see that," she argued. "Feeling pain and sadness for someone you've lost is good because it means they're still a part of you. They're still here." She pushed her hand over his heart this time. "Missing someone means they left their mark on this world and the people in it and I happen to think that's a pretty incredible thing."

Ethan chewed his lip. "I guess."

Chloe smiled. "It may sound silly, but when I miss my Grandpa I like to think I'm here remembering him and he's somewhere remembering me. It makes me feel kind of special to have him watching over me all the time. More loved, ya know?"

"I don't know if I believe in that," Ethan said.

"I can respect that." Chloe smiled. "But, one thing I know for sure is that if my grandpa is watching me, he'd be pretty upset if he knew he was the reason I wasn't smiling."

Chloe saw a spark of emotion in Ethan's eyes. "So would my mother."

"My grandpa used to say, Co-Co, you've got a smile that could end famine. Don't go wasting it on a frown." She laughed. "Whatever that means."

Ethan's hands found their way to Chloe's face. "Your grandfather was right," he said, tenderly. "Your smile is more than enough to live on."

Chloe swallowed hard. Ethan's lips were so close to hers that the heat of their breath tangled into one bright cloud. Chloe watched the cloud of steam dance between them, wondering how on earth she was still breathing when everything in her body felt frozen with anticipation. She licked her lips, shivering with nerves at the thought of Ethan's kiss. She closed her eyes but instead of his kiss, Chloe was met with a snowball to the back of the head.

"Ow!" She stumbled forward and Ethan caught her. "Hey!" she yelled seeing Brady, Margot and Owen charging toward them with armfuls of snowballs.

Ethan grabbed her hand. "Run!"

25

Ethan

THE NEXT HOUR was spent sprinting through the woods and hurling packed balls of snow at Owen, Margot and Brady. Eventually, Margot and Owen paired up, leaving Brady on his own, something Ethan was happy to exploit. He pegged the jock-wad more than a few times, each time easing the jealousy he felt in the pit of his stomach knowing Brady's lips had once touched Chloe's.

She was far too good for a guy like Brady. *Probably far too good for Ethan, too.* But he was taking one thing at a time. And right now he was enjoying beaming Brady with snowballs and holding Chloe's hand as they dashed through the woods.

Chloe

. . .

CHLOE WAS EXHAUSTED when Ethan pulled her behind a fallen tree. She doubled over trying to catch her breath from laughter and excursion. She was covered from head to toe in snow. She didn't know how there was any left on the ground after their epic snowball battle.

"I can't breathe," she gasped between laughter.

"Shhh," Ethan teased, pushing his finger to her lips. "They'll hear us."

Chloe immediately stopped laughing as Ethan's finger lingered on her lower lip. Her breath caught in her throat as she realized she didn't care who heard her. That tiny bit of contact ignited a fire inside her that threatened to engulf her if she didn't give in to what she wanted right now.

She reached up and pulled Ethan's face closer to hers. Their lips met, slowly at first, but then their kiss erupted into an electric sizzle that made her chest burn from the inside out. *How did kissing him always manage to get better?*

He was oxygen to her flames, kindling to her fire. She didn't care that her lungs ached from lack of air. She didn't need to breathe as much as she needed this kiss.

Ethan pulled away, his eyes wide, chest heaving. But Chloe wasn't ready to stop yet. She moved to pull him back but he stiffened.

"Chloe . . ." he breathed.

There was warning in his voice, but longing too. And something more. There was always something more he was holding back. "Why don't you ever say what you're thinking?" she asked.

He shook his head. "Because I don't want to scare you off."

"Maybe I don't scare that easily," she challenged.

Ethan's hand rubbed the tension from his jaw as he wrestled with his thoughts. "Everyone scares, Chloe."

"I'm not everyone."

He stopped his fidgeting and looked at her. "No, you most certainly are not."

She took a tentative step closer. "Do you not want me to kiss you?"

"No! That's not it at all. I think . . . I think I want you to kiss me more than anything in this world."

A slow smile spread across her face. "That doesn't sound so scary to me."

"That's not the problem, Chloe. The problem is that I'm a mess. I'm no good for you. And this," he gestured between them, "will never work."

"How can you possibly know that?"

"Because I won't make it easy. You've barely scratched the surface of my issues. I'm not an easy person to love."

"Maybe you should let me be the judge of that."

His mouth opened, then shut. Again, he stopped the words that were clawing to get out. Watching him hold back was insufferable. Chloe wanted to climb inside him and see everything he was hiding. She needed to chase away her doubts because she was pretty sure that he felt exactly the same way she did, but she didn't want to be wrong again. She didn't want to let herself get hurt like Brady had hurt her. "Ethan, please tell me what you're thinking."

"I'm thinking you shouldn't say that kind of thing."

"What kind of thing? That I could love you?"

Anger flared across his face before it melted into agony. "Yes," he hissed. "I'm not easy to love, Chloe."

She took a step closer. "You said that already. I'm not scared."

"I am," he whispered.

Ethan looked at her then with so much fear in his gorgeous heartbroken eyes that it left Chloe breathless. She feared she could drown in the stormy green ocean of his eyes. But when he pulled her into his arms and kissed her, the tumultuous sea calmed and Chloe realized that she could never drown when it came to Ethan. She was his lifeboat. *All she had to do was get him to trust her enough to climb in.*

Bliss stole over her as Ethan clung to her, his kisses deepening. She'd never felt this type of completion in her life. He needed her and she loved something about that so much. She'd always felt that she was the needy one. It was why she was so lost when Margot left and Brady dumped her. Chloe had never felt necessary, but with Ethan, she felt strong, vital even. The way he clung to her with such unrestrained passion made her never want to let go.

With him, she felt more like herself than she ever had. She was no longer a lone bookend, slipping away. Ethan gave her something to hold onto. They'd both been falling, but together they held each other up. Together they were whole.

Sadly, Chloe didn't get a chance to convey any of that to Ethan. Their passionate kiss ended much too soon, interrupted by Margot's gasp.

"Oh!" Margot inhaled sharply, snowball still raised in her hand. "I didn't realize . . . I . . . um." She stuttered over her words and finally looked at her watch. "I think we should go. Mom and Dad texted. They need help at the lodge."

Chloe's cheeks burned. She wished Margot hadn't found her kissing Ethan like that. She'd only yesterday promised her sister no more secrets and here she was kissing Margot's boyfriend's brother. And from the stunned look on Margot's face, she wasn't happy about it.

Before Chloe could even attempt to say anything Margot dropped her snowball and ran back toward the snowmobiles. Chloe heard the engines sputter to life a minute later and her heart sank, taking the euphoric kiss she'd just shared with Ethan with it.

"Are you okay?" he asked, quietly.

"Yeah." She smiled up at him and linking their gloved fingers. "Ready to head back?"

He kissed her cheek, sending warmth through her whole body. “If we must.”

She laughed. “I think we must before we thaw this whole forest,” she teased, feeling the feverish flush her cheeks still held. “But this,” she said, gesturing between them, “is just a pause.”

“I think I like the sound of that.”

26

Ethan

THE SNOWBALL WAR went on so long that there wasn't time for Chloe to teach Ethan how to drive the snowmobile. But he didn't mind. He actually preferred riding on the back with his arms looped securely around her waist. He couldn't imagine wanting to be anywhere else. He loved the feel of her soft hair lashing his cheeks and the way she leaned into him a bit more whenever he squeezed her thighs.

He took in the snowy landscape that rushed by, noticing that everything looked brighter and more beautiful somehow. He knew he had Chloe to thank for that. Being with her made everything better.

As they neared her house, Ethan noticed a flash of sunlight reflecting off the surface of the pond. "Hey, look at that."

Chloe slowed the sled to see where he was pointing.

"Is that the pond you used to ice skate on?"

Chloe nodded. “Yep.”

“It looks frozen.”

He caught her smile as she turned her head to look closer. “Wow, you’re right. That hasn’t happened in years. The temperature must’ve dropped pretty low last night.”

Ethan laughed. “Why do you sound surprised by that? It’s freaking freezing right now.”

Chloe snorted. “Oh, Manhattan. This is nothing.”

She gunned the snowmobile and they rocketed across the snow, turning the light snowfall into a blur of icy needles that stung any exposed skin. Surprisingly, Ethan didn’t care. He just gripped Chloe tighter, letting her laughter warm him all the way through.

Chloe

CHLOE’S PARENTS were rushing out the door when she and Ethan walked up to the front porch. She let Ethan go inside ahead of her and hung back to talk to her parents.

“Hi, honey,” her mother said. “We’ve gotta do some last minute prep for the wedding. Lunch is on the table. Can you meet us at the lodge after you’ve eaten? We could use the extra help with the wedding today.”

“Of course.”

“Thanks, sweetheart.”

Chloe was overcome with the urge to hug her mother, so she did. “I love you, Mom.”

It felt so good to have her mother’s familiar arms around her. This was the first time Chloe had seen her parents since Ethan told her about losing his.

Her mother’s shock was evident as she hugged Chloe back,

slowly at first, until the embrace turned fierce. "I love you too, sweetheart."

Her mother pulled back and gave Chloe a look of concern. "Is everything okay?"

"Everything's great, Mom," she replied. "I just realized I don't say I love you as much as I should."

Her parents exchanged a worried glance, but that didn't stop Chloe from giving her father a giant hug, too. "Love you, Dad."

"I love you, baby girl."

She kissed her father on the cheek and pulled away. "I'll see you at the lodge in an hour."

As Chloe turned to go inside, she heard her parents whispering to each other, wondering what all the hugging was about. It made Chloe happy and sad at the same time. Hugging her parents and telling them she loved them was such a simple gesture, but that fact that it caused them alarm meant she didn't do it nearly enough. She made a mental note to change that.

Chloe walked inside, instantly hit by the stifling heat of the roaring fire. She stripped off her layers and headed upstairs to change. Taking a deep breath, she readied herself to face her sister.

It was time to smooth things over with Margot.

27

Chloe

MARGOT WAS SITTING at Chloe's vanity, brushing the snow out of her hair when Chloe walked in.

"Hey," Chloe greeted, sitting on the bed behind her.

Margot's eyes met Chloe's in the mirror. "Hey."

"About me and Ethan . . ."

Margot turned around, her eyes wide. "So, I wasn't hallucinating? You were really kissing him?"

Chloe nodded.

"Co-Co, if your plan is to make Brady jealous, I get it, but don't use Ethan, okay? I'll help you find another way."

"I don't want Brady back."

Margot frowned. "You don't?"

"I want Ethan," Chloe said, surprised how easily she'd admitted that. She watched her reflection in the mirror and liked how confident she looked after that statement.

Margot stood up and walked over to the bed. She sat next to Chloe and took her hand. "Co-Co, Ethan and Owen . . . they've been through a lot."

"I know."

Margot's pretty face scrunched in confusion. "You do?"

"I know about Ethan's mom," she said. "He told me last night."

Margot's deep hazel eyes held a strange hope. "He talked to you about his mom?"

Chloe nodded and watched relief sweep through her sister.

"Chloe, I don't know if you realize how incredible that is. Owen has been so worried about him."

That made Chloe's eyes widen. "Owen's worried about Ethan?"

"Of course."

"Then why wasn't he the one watching *Miracle on 34th Street* with Ethan last night?"

Margot chewed her lip, looking agitated. "Is that what you two were doing on the couch?"

Chloe nodded.

Margot sighed. "Owen told me Ethan wasn't going to do that this year."

"You knew about it?" Chloe couldn't believe Margot had known and did nothing to make her boyfriend and Ethan feel better. That wasn't like her at all.

Margot sighed. "Chloe, Ethan and Owen have a very different relationship than we do. They love each other, but they deal with things differently. Owen has trouble dealing with his grief, but he manages it in his own way. And Ethan . . . the only person he's ever opened up about his feelings to is Owen, but it's too much for Owen to handle all the time. He doesn't know how to help Ethan when he's hurting so much himself."

"So he just ignores his brother?"

Margot frowned. "I don't understand it myself really. I just try to be there for Owen when he lets me. He's very private about his family. He only just told me about his mother a few weeks ago."

"That's why you invited them here for Christmas, isn't it?"

"Yes, it's one of the reasons," Margot said, wringing her hands in her lap.

Chloe mulled it over. Margot's cryptic reply and nervous hand-wringing was making Chloe think there might be even more that she still needed to learn about the Hall boys. But either way, she was glad they were here. "I'm glad you brought them home with you, Go-Go."

"Me too," Margot said, squeezing Chloe's hand. "I don't know how they dealt with so much for so long. It makes me count my blessings."

"Yeah, me too."

"I'm glad Ethan is talking to you, Chloe. I know he needs someone in his life. And if it can't be Owen right now, I'm glad it's you."

"You are?"

"Of course."

"So, you're not mad that I like him?"

"Why would I be mad?"

"I don't know. Isn't it a little weird?"

"Why? Because he's in college?"

"That and because you're dating his very similar-looking brother."

"Life is short, little sister. When you find the good ones you gotta hold onto them."

"How do you know the good ones?" *She'd thought Brady was good.*

Margot grinned. "You just know."

Chloe rolled her eyes. "That's helpful."

Margot laughed. "It's hard to explain, but you'll know it when you feel it. Trust me."

Chloe smiled. She *did* trust her sister. And she knew Margot would never throw that phrase around lightly. "I do trust you. I just wish there was more we could do for them."

"I know. Ethan and Owen are really good guys. I don't know what I would've done without them in the city. They really took me under their wing. And I know they're brothers but I'm learning they're just as different as you and me. Owen is so happy and full of life, and he just makes me smile all the time. I feel like Ethan could be that way too if he would just let someone in. Owen worries about him a lot."

"I think it would help Ethan if he knew that."

Margot got a wistful look in her eyes. "Maybe, but sometimes I think people need to find their own way back to each other."

Chloe nodded. "But it might not be the worst thing if we helped them connect a little. I know how bad it would hurt if you and I grew apart."

Margot chewed her lip. "Co-Co, I'm really sorry I wasn't there for you with Brady. It must've been awful."

"It's okay."

"No, it's not. You're my sister and I love you more than anything in the world. I want to be the one you call with the good news *and* the bad news."

"Me too," Chloe said, letting her sister pull her into a fierce embrace.

"I love you, Chloe."

"I love you, too."

They laughed when they noticed how puffy their eyes were from the all tears they shed while they hugged each other.

"These boys are turning us into a bunch of saps," Chloe joked.

Margot's eyes fell to her lap and she began to wring her hands again.

"What's wrong, Go-Go?"

"There might be another reason I'm a little more emotional than usual."

Chloe's eyes widened as she watched her sister's hand move to her stomach.

"I'm pregnant," Margot whispered.

"What?" Chloe screeched.

"Shhh!"

"Are you sure?" Chloe asked, still not sure she was able to wrap her brain around what Margot was saying.

"Of course I'm sure. I took like a gazillion tests."

"Oh my God, Margot. This is . . . I don't even know," Chloe replied, shock making her thoughts scatter. "What are you going to do?"

"I don't know. I only found out a few days before we came home. I haven't even told Owen yet."

"What? You have to tell him!"

"I know, but I wanted to wait until the holidays were over. He has so much to deal with emotionally this time of year and I thought adding something like this on top of it wouldn't be a good idea."

Margot's hands were shaking. Chloe grabbed them. "Go-Go, I'm here for you. Whatever you need."

Tears began leaking out of Margot's big hazel eyes. "I don't know what I'm going to do."

"What do you want to do?" Chloe asked.

Margot's hands cradled her flat stomach. "I want to have this baby." She sniffled. "Mom and Dad are going to kill me."

"No they won't, Margot."

"Chloe, I'm only twenty-one. I still have more than a year of college to finish."

"So. A baby doesn't mean you can't finish school. And you're a year older than Mom was when she had you."

Margot sighed. "I know. But things were different then. Mom didn't go to college. Besides, I don't even know if Owen wants kids. We've never talked about it and it's not like he's had a very good example of family in his life."

"Maybe he'll be happy to have a chance to have his own family," Chloe offered.

"Maybe . . . but I'm guessing he probably didn't plan on starting one at twenty-one."

Margot hung her head and Chloe pulled her sister into a hug. "You just need to talk to him, Go-Go."

"I'm so afraid I'll lose him. I love him so much, Chloe. I've never felt this way about anyone before. He makes everyday of my life the greatest one yet. And all I wanted to do was love him back that same way. I wanted to make his life better, but now I've complicated everything. I don't know what I'm going to do."

Chloe stroked her sister's hair while she sobbed. Chloe's problems had never felt so small. All she had to complain about was work and being dumped by a boy she wasn't even sure she should've dated in the first place. That was nothing compared to what Ethan and Owen and Margot were dealing with. The boys were faced with a holiday that reminded them how little family they had left in the world, while Margot was faced with starting her own family way before she was ready.

Before Christmas break, Chloe never could've imagined she was the one with nothing to complain about, but that certainly seemed to be the case. She didn't mind, though. She actually liked feeling like the glue for a change. She was a keeper of secrets, a shoulder to cry on, an anchor in the storm. She felt a tremendous pressure in her chest to help everyone, but she also felt her heart gladly answer the calling. She wanted to help.

Helping others was what she wanted to dedicate her life to

and right now her sister needed her help. "Margot, it's going to be okay."

"How?"

"I don't know, but I promise you it is. Trust me, okay?"

Margot's eyes watered as she caught the significance of Chloe's words. It was a phrase they only used with utmost certainty. And although Chloe wasn't sure exactly how the next few days would go, she knew that things would be okay. Because she would be there for her sister, no matter what.

Chloe took Margot's hand. "Come on. Let's go get you some lunch."

Margot sniffled and wiped her eyes. "Then what?"

"Then we'll figure the rest out as we go."

28

Ethan

ETHAN FOUND himself bartending at the lodge after lunch. When they'd walked into the massive lobby he'd been greeted by a cacophony of Christmas cheer. There were Christmas carolers, wedding guests and people who'd just come to experience the magical holiday spirit that the Price family had somehow managed to capture.

At first, Ethan thought it would all be too much, but with Chloe by his side, he felt surprisingly calm. Something had changed in her since their last kiss. There was a quiet confidence in her that reassured him in a way he couldn't explain. And when her mother came running up begging for help with the wedding, he'd been eager to pitch in.

Apparently, some of the employees couldn't make it up the steep hill to the lodge for their shift thanks to the icy road conditions. That left them a bartender short at the wedding.

They were also short a few servers. Chloe told her mother not to worry and handed out the ugly staff Christmas sweaters along with tasks that needed to be covered.

Margot and Owen were assigned server duties, while Ethan and Chloe ended up tending bar. The only drink he really knew how to make was an Old Fashioned. His grandmother taught him how to make them when he was young. He could do it in his sleep.

Luckily, most of the wedding guests just wanted beer or wine. And whenever anyone asked for a more complicated cocktail, Chloe had his back.

"You should really try the guest bartender's special," she'd say with a wink in Ethan's direction. "It's a top secret recipe from Manhattan."

Ethan felt his guard slipping the more time he spent with Chloe and her family. They made it easy for him to feel included. And as he and Chloe fell into a comfortable routine behind the bar, Ethan couldn't help getting caught up in the joy of the winter wedding. It filled him with an overwhelming feeling of something rare—*hope.*

Chloe

MARGOT CAME HUSTLING over to the bar with Owen at her side. "Dad needs us to pick up the ice sculpture from town. The company was supposed to deliver it here for the Christmas Eve party tonight but they couldn't make it up to the lodge in this weather. It's at the postal center in town but the post master thinks it'll melt if we don't pick it up soon." Anxiety edged Margot's voice. "Can you cover the floor for us, while we take the plow truck into town?"

Chloe frowned. "You can't lift an ice sculpture, Go-Go."

Margot's eyes widened with fear over her secret.

"Hey, this here is the strongest woman I know," Owen teased, pinching Margot's thin arms. "But your sis is right, babe. Why don't you let Ethan come with me instead?"

The worry Chloe felt for her sister softened when she saw the sweet way Owen doted on her.

"But you don't know where you're going," Margot argued.

"Just put the address in my phone."

Chloe turned to Ethan while Margot pulled up the GPS on Owen's phone. "Do you mind going with Owen?" she asked, quietly.

"Not at all."

Chloe squeezed his hand. "I'll see ya at the party."

After the boys left, Chloe pulled her sister aside behind the bar. "So, did you tell Owen?"

Margot shook her head. "Not yet."

"Margot!"

"I'll do it tonight. I want to do it somewhere quiet so we can talk."

"Okay. I can sleep on the couch tonight so you have the room to yourself."

"I'm not going to kick you out of your room, Chloe."

"You're not kicking me out. I'm offering. You need to talk to Owen. You're a bundle of nerves and that isn't good for you or the baby."

Margot tugged at a loose thread on her sweater sleeve. "You don't think I should just wait until after Christmas?"

"No! You need to tell him."

"But what if he freaks out and I ruin Christmas?"

"What if he doesn't freak out and you give him the best Christmas gift ever?"

Margot let a small smile tug at her lips. "You think?"

"You'll never know if you don't talk to him."

"Okay." Margot squeezed Chloe's hands. "You're right. This

could be good. I'll talk to him tonight." She pulled Chloe into a tight hug. "Thanks, Co-Co. You're going to be the best aunt ever."

That simple sentence sent Chloe's heart into overdrive. *She was going to be an aunt!* She hadn't even thought of that. She hugged her sister back fiercely, praying her news would fill Owen with as much love as she felt for her sister in that moment.

29

Ethan

"So," Owen said as he concentrated on the road. "You doing okay?"

Ethan looked at his brother, surprised he was asking. Owen liked to discuss his feelings even less than Ethan did. Their inability to deal with the fall out of their mother's death and father's abandonment had created a divide between them, making it hard for Ethan to know how to answer Owen's question.

If he said he was fine, that would be the end of the discussion. But Ethan didn't want it to end. He craved a way to connect with his brother the way they used to. But he feared if he said too much it would push Owen away.

Ethan decided to tread lightly. "I've actually felt a little better than I expected to feel today."

Owen gave him a tight smile. "Good. Me too."

"Good," Ethan replied, kicking himself for being so bad at this.

He found himself wishing Chloe were sitting next to him. It was surprisingly easy to open up when she was around. Ethan was about to say that he was glad Owen dragged him up here for the holidays when Owen spoke again.

"I want to ask you something, E."

Ethan tried to read the tension in his brother's expression. "Okay."

"I want to ask Margot to move in with me next semester."

Ethan blinked waiting for more. "That's not a question."

Owen exhaled his frustration. "I guess I'm asking if you'd be okay with that?"

"Are you asking if she can live with us or are you asking me to move out?"

Owen took his eyes off the road. "I'd never ask you to move out, E. You're my brother."

Those words slammed into Ethan's heart, splintering the thick layer of scar tissue that sealed it off from the world.

'You're my brother.'

'I'd never ask you to move out.'

Owen's words circled around Ethan's heart until his chest felt so tight he couldn't breathe.

Sensing Ethan's stress, Owen eased the massive plow truck into a snow-covered parking lot and put it in park. "Ethan," he said. "Look at me."

He couldn't. If he did he'd lose it. His conversations with Chloe the past few days had left his emotions too close to the surface and now his brother was pulling at the the last remaining thread holding him together.

"Ethan, I know I'm no good at this," Owen continued. "I know I'm no substitute for Mom or even Dad, but I really do try." He rubbed his hand over his mouth as he blew out an exasperated breath. "I'm trying to tell you that I care, E. I'm here for you. I know I haven't done the best job of it in the past. I guess I just wasn't any good at dealing with my emotions myself, so I didn't know how to help you with yours, but Margot has changed all of that. She just makes everything easier." He sighed. "I don't even know how, but she does. She makes me want to be a better person. And I need to start being a better brother."

Ethan met Owen's eyes and for the first time, he felt he truly knew what his older brother meant. Because Ethan felt it, too—with Chloe. She was like a piece of him that he'd never known he was missing. And it was crazy that they'd only just met because he had such a strong attachment to her. He just wanted to hold her close and never let go. So of course Ethan understood Owen wanting to do the same with Margot.

Owen sighed heavily. "Look, I know Margot isn't your favorite person in the world, but I was hoping after this weekend you might see that living with her could be fun."

Ethan laughed. "That's one word for it." His affection for Chloe *did* make Margot more tolerable but Ethan didn't think he'd ever say living with Margot would be his idea of fun.

Owen's mouth twisted into a smile. "I know she's a little chipper for your taste."

"Chipper? She makes a chipmunk look like a lazy, lump of depression."

Owen laughed, shaking his head. "I swear, if we could find a way to bottle her energy we'd be millionaires."

"We *are* millionaires," Ethan teased.

Owen's eyes turned serious again. "I thought you didn't want to touch any of Mom's money?"

"I don't."

Owen was quiet for a minute. "She left it to us, E. Adopted or not, we were her kids. That's all that should matter."

Ethan nodded, his stomach knotting at the mention of their trust fund. Their grandmother had fought hard to make sure that their father didn't get his hands on it, but even after winning that court battle, Ethan had wanted nothing to do with his mother's fortune. He didn't feel it was rightfully his. Maybe their father was right. Maybe they didn't deserve it more than he did. They weren't really her children by blood. A piece of paper from the state didn't change that.

The only reason Ethan hadn't just given it all away to his mother's charity was because the trust was in Owen's name as well. And Owen stubbornly said he wouldn't take the money if Ethan didn't.

Currently, they only lived off the interest, using it to pay tuition, room and board. *Was this why Owen was bringing it up? Did he want to use the money to get them a bigger apartment so Margot could move in?*

"If you want to live with Margot, I want you to," Ethan finally said.

Owen studied him quietly. "You're sure?"

"Yes."

"And what about you?"

"What about me?" Ethan asked.

"I want you to live with us, if you're okay with that. If not, I won't ask Margot to move in." Owen smirked a little. "I don't even know if she'll say yes. She seems pretty happy at the sorority house."

Ethan laughed. "She'll say yes."

"You think?"

"Of course. She's disgustingly in love with you."

Owen got a dopey grin on his face. "God, I hope so."

"You love her, huh?"

Owen nodded. "Like I never imagined. I'd propose tomorrow if we weren't so young."

Ethan smiled. He liked seeing his brother this happy. Owen always looked happy, but usually Ethan was watching that happiness from the outside, looking in. Now, he felt like Owen was allowing him to be a part of his joy. Or maybe Ethan was the one finally allowing himself to be a part of it. "I'm glad she makes you happy. I think you should ask her to move in. But I think we'll need a bigger place."

Owen nodded. "Done." His grin was so wide it made Ethan smile.

Owen squeezed his shoulder. "Thank you, brother."

"You're welcome, brother."

"We're gonna be okay, ya know?"

Ethan nodded and for the first time, he started to believe it was true.

30

Ethan

ETHAN GLANCED AT THE CLOCK. It took longer than he thought to load the massive ice sculpture and the little shopping detour Ethan suggested didn't help matters. Plus, they had to stop back at the house to change for the party.

By the time, Ethan followed his brother into the barn, the party was in full swing. The word 'barn' also didn't do the space justice. He liked how the Price family seemed hell bent on underwhelming people by calling their five star hotel a lodge and the gorgeous storefront a barn.

The *barn* was beautifully decorated for Christmas. There were trees, wreaths and pine garland strung with lights everywhere he looked. He loved the simple red and black buffalo plaid that gave the cocktail tables a rustic feel. Even the pine dance floor looked inviting with the party-goers dancing to the live band.

Ethan took in the gorgeous scene wondering if he could ever accurately describe the beauty of the barn party to someone who hadn't experienced it. But his musings were cut short when he saw Chloe. The breathtaking Christmas scene didn't hold a candle to the vision walking across the dance floor.

Chloe was wearing a long evergreen dress with her long hair down around her shoulders. It looked like silk and Ethan could scarcely think of anything but running his fingers through it.

She walked right up to him, not shy about her glowing smile. "Hey you."

"Hey yourself." Ethan stared at her, searching for just the right words. "You look . . ." *like the most beautiful thing in the room, Chloe*. He shook his head, knowing better than to admit his true feelings. "Very nice."

She grinned. "Thanks. You look pretty nice, yourself. I was starting to worry about you."

"You were?"

"Yeah, you guys were gone a long time. Did everything go okay with the ice sculpture?"

Right on cue two guys dressed in lodge sweaters wheeled the massive reindeer into the barn. "Yeah." He nodded to the ice sculpture. "Owen was just being cautious. The roads were pretty icy."

"Good. I'm glad you were being careful."

Ethan stared at Chloe's shy smile. *Are you worrying about me, Chloe?*

"Do you want to dance?" she asked.

With you? More than anything. He gave a slight nod. "Okay."

Chloe led him to the dance floor and once Ethan had her in his arms he didn't want to let go. He found himself wondering how on earth he'd ever survived without spending every moment of his life with his arms around this girl. *And even worse, how was he going to manage to let go when Christmas came to an end?*

Ethan swayed to the music, letting Chloe do most of the leading. He couldn't seem to do more than run his fingers through her hair.

"I like your hair like this," he whispered. "You should wear it down more often."

"Ethan Hall, are you commenting on my hairstyle? You'd better be careful."

"Why's that?"

"You're starting to sound like a boyfriend."

He laughed. "Is that so?"

"Definitely."

"Well, I guess I will have to take your word for it since I've never been a boyfriend before."

Chloe shook her head. "I still don't know if I believe you. You are definitely boyfriend material."

"Boyfriend material, huh? For who?"

Before Chloe could answer Brady suddenly appeared. He wore a grin that Ethan wanted to wipe off his face. "Hey, Chloe. You owe me a dance."

She frowned. "I do?"

"Sixth grade, you got chicken pox and I had to go to the dance all by myself. You said you'd make it up to me. Well, this is me calling in that dance." Brady looked right at Ethan and winked. "You don't mind, right bro?"

Of course he minded but once again Ethan kept his emotions in check and stepped away from Chloe without a word.

Brady

. . .

A NEW SONG STARTED, its pace a little faster than what Brady would've preferred. But Chloe didn't even seem to notice that they were the only two slow dancing to a fast song. Her eyes were still on Ethan. She'd watched him walk away with a longing in her eyes that Brady was familiar with.

He'd seen that look before. The way Chloe was watching Ethan . . . it was the same way she used to watch Brady. A knot formed in the pit of his stomach. *Was he too late?* No. He refused to believe it. He and Chloe had a history. He just needed to make her remember.

Brady tucked a long strand of hair behind Chloe's ear. "Clo?"

"Hmm?"

"I was saying you look beautiful tonight." He'd said it once already but it was as if she hadn't heard him at all. She felt like a mannequin in his arms.

"Oh, thanks."

"I had a great time snowmobiling today."

She smiled at him but not the way she used to. "Yeah, today was fun."

"Maybe we can hang out tomorrow?"

"Tomorrow's Christmas, Brady."

"So. We always used to hang out on Christmas."

Chloe bit her lip. She was looking at him now, but he wished she wasn't. "Brady, things aren't like they were before."

"What do you mean? I thought we were friends again."

"We are. And I'll always love our friendship, Brady, but I don't want to go back to how it was before."

"Back to being my girlfriend you mean?"

She nodded. "I'm sorry. I didn't mean to lead you on. I wasn't really sure how I felt at first, but now . . ." She paused and glanced over Brady's shoulder again. He followed her eyes to where they landed on Ethan. "Now, I just feel like we're not as right for each other as I thought."

"Because of him?" Brady asked, jutting his chin in Ethan's direction.

"I don't know."

"It's okay, Chloe. I'm not mad. All of this is my fault. I'm the one who screwed up and let you go."

"Maybe you didn't screw up. Maybe we weren't meant to be more than we are."

Brady tried to smile but he felt a dull ache in his chest as his hopes deflated. "Well, if the next guy screws up maybe we'll find out."

"Maybe."

"Make sure he treats you better than I did," Brady said, kissing her on the cheek. "Merry Christmas, Chloe."

"Merry Christmas, Brady."

With a sigh, Brady let his arms fall away from Chloe. His heart felt heavy as he turned to walk away. Maybe she was right. Maybe they weren't meant to be more. Either way, it looked like he wouldn't find out. Chloe didn't want to give him another chance. And he really couldn't blame her.

Brady stuffed his hands in his pockets as he walked off the dance floor. When he passed Ethan he frowned. Brady wanted to hate the guy, he really did, but as he'd said to Chloe, this was Brady's fault, not Ethan's.

Brady gave Ethan a sad smile and clapped a hand on his shoulder. "Good luck." Then he walked away.

Brady found himself wondering if maybe he should've hung a different wish on the Christmas tree yesterday. Instead of wishing to find something he'd lost, he should've wished for knowledge. Because if he'd known what he had in the first place, he never would have let it go.

31

Chloe

CHLOE DIDN'T WASTE a moment before seeking out Ethan. She'd made sure never to lose sight of him the whole time she was with Brady. After their conversation she finally felt free. It made her feel like she was walking on air as she approached Ethan. Unlike Brady, Chloe knew a good thing when she had it and she had no intention of letting anyone else interrupt her before she let Ethan know exactly what was in her heart.

Ethan

ETHAN'S HEART was his throat as he watched Chloe walk toward him. She was smiling so he prayed he'd misinterpreted Brady's comment. But it was hard to feel hopeful. From where Ethan had been standing while Brady danced with the girl who'd captured Ethan's heart, it looked every bit like Chloe was getting back together with her ex.

Please don't break my heart, Chloe. You don't have to pick me but you can do so much better than him.

"Hey," Chloe greeted cheerfully when she reached Ethan. "Can we finish our dance?"

He nodded.

For a while all they did was dance, but Ethan found it impossible to enjoy himself like he had been before. Each time a new song started he wondered if it would be the song he was listening to when Chloe dashed all of his dreams.

Finally, he couldn't take it anymore. "Chloe," he said, quietly. "I need to ask you something."

"Okay."

"Are you over Brady? Because I'm certain he's not over you."

She sighed. "Maybe he's not, but that doesn't matter. He's not the one I want to be with."

Hope spiked through Ethan, sending his pulse through the roof. "Really?"

"Really. I'm not interested in repeating past mistakes."

Ethan huffed a quiet laugh. "Harsh."

Chloe laughed, too. "I let him down easy. Besides, I think Brady will be just fine."

"How do you know?"

Chloe jutted her chin toward the bar.

When Ethan followed her line of sight he shook his head. Brady was already flirting with another girl. "Wow, it seems you made the right decision."

Chloe

. . .

Chloe sighed. "Brady's always been like a puppy with a new toy. I don't think he can help it." She laughed. "He just prefers things that are shiny and new."

Her heart hurt a little, realizing at some point she'd lost that appeal. *Would that happen with Ethan?*

"What are you thinking?" Ethan asked, his lips so close to her ear that she shivered.

"I guess I'm just wondering if everyone's sparkle dulls at some point."

"What makes you say that?"

"I guess that's what happened with me and Brady."

Ethan pulled back and stunned Chloe with an angry gaze. "Sometimes I feel like we're on the exact same wavelength and sometimes you're ridiculously blind." Ethan stroked a hand slowly down her cheek. "There is nothing dull about you, Chloe Price." His hand trailed to her chest, pressing over her heart. "Your sparkle is right here. Anyone too blind to see that doesn't deserve you anyway."

Chloe swallowed against the fever threatening to engulf her. No one had ever said something that beautiful to her in her entire life. She never even knew she'd been waiting to hear those words but now that she had she felt like she was falling toward the earth without a parachute.

That was it. Those words pushed her over the edge. Chloe was no longer falling for Ethan. She was head over heels plummeting. She was seconds away from letting her lips crash into his when something buzzed against her hip making her jump.

"What's wrong?"

Chloe blinked back to reality and realized it was her phone buzzing wildly in the deep pocket of her flowy dress. "Sorry," she murmured.

Normally, Chloe wouldn't have even brought her phone but she was worried about Margot. Her sister had been a complete mess the entire time the boys were gone, oscillating between fits of sobs and laughter. Chloe had taken her back to the house and made her lay down. She seemed better before they came to the party, but she said she'd been feeling queasy. Chloe chalked it up to nerves, but she told Margot she'd have her phone handy in case she needed anything.

So when Chloe saw her sister's name on her screen, followed by a cryptic text, her heart plummeted.

Margot: 911. Meet me in the ladies room.

Chloe reached up and kissed Ethan on the lips.

He blinked at her in shock. "Please hold that thought."

As she started to pull away he grabbed her hand, following her off the dance floor. "Wait. Where are you going?"

"Margot needs me."

"Why? What's wrong?"

"It's private." Chloe hated the look that crossed Ethan's face when she told him she had to exclude him. "Can I see your phone?" she asked quickly.

He pulled it from his pocket and Chloe swiped it from his hand, rushing to put her number in. Her fingers flew across the screen until she sent herself a text. When she felt her phone vibrate in her pocket she reached up and kissed Ethan again. "I'm sorry, but I have to go. I'll text you later and explain. I promise."

32

Chloe

CHLOE RACED to the ladies room, finding Margot doubled over in a stall. She quickly locked the door and ran to her sister. "Margot? What's wrong?"

"I don't know. I think I ate something bad. One minute I was dancing with Owen the next . . ." She paused her story to wretch into the toilet again. "Oh my God. What if I have food poisoning? Will that hurt the baby?"

Chloe grabbed a paper towel and ran it under the sink, handing it to Margot so she could wipe her mouth. "I don't think it's food poisoning, Go-Go."

"You don't?"

"It's probably morning sickness."

"But it's the middle of the night."

Chloe smiled. "It can happen at any time."

"What? How do you know that?"

"Because Aunt Chloe is going to be a nurse," she said, proudly.

Margot's eyes bulged and she wretched again. When she turned back she had tears in her eyes. They left streaks of mascara down her cheeks. "I'm going to be a terrible mother, Co-Co. I don't know anything about babies."

Chloe pulled her sister into her arms and rubbed her back. "You'll learn. And I'm pretty sure every first-time mother says that."

"Really?"

"Really."

CHLOE SPENT the rest of the night holding Margot's hair back while she got sick. Luckily, she got her back to the house between bouts of nausea so Margot at least could get comfortable. After checking all her sister's vitals and asking her what she'd eaten, Chloe was positive it was nothing more serious than morning sickness.

She gave her sister a jug of water and a packet of saltines. Once Margot fell asleep, Chloe felt her mind wander back to Ethan. The last she'd seen of him he'd been watching her rush off. He'd looked so confused. Chloe hated that she was making this awful time of year even more confusing for him. That wasn't her intention at all. In fact, if he felt the way she did, and she suspected he did, she planned to make his holiday a whole lot better. She just needed a solid uninterrupted evening with him.

An idea sparked to life and Chloe grabbed her phone. She quickly fired off a text to Ethan.

Her: Hi. Sorry I had to rush out earlier.

Him: That's okay. Is everything okay with Margot?

Her: It will be.

Him: Where are you?

Her: In my room with Margot. Where are you?

Him: Still at the party. Should I come home?

Her: Stay, enjoy yourself.

Him: Kinda hard without you.

Chloe smiled like a fool.

Him: Want me to come home?

Her: No. I'm still taking care of Margot.

Him: What's wrong with her?

Chloe thought about that for a moment. The last thing she wanted to do was lie to Ethan, but it wasn't her place to share Margot's news. Chloe decided on a half truth.

Her: Female issues.

Him: Enough said.

Her: There's something I want to say to you but it needs to be in person. Can we continue our conversation tonight?

Him: Same time, same place?

Her: You read my mind.

Chloe added a smiley face.

Him: Looking forward to it.

Ethan sent back a winking face.

Chloe giggled. She loved that his emoji was smiling. It meant there was hope for him. Maybe she'd found a way to make him smile on the inside. That was progress. And with any luck, after tonight, they'd both be smiling.

Margot stirred in bed. She opened her eyes and looked at Chloe. "What are you so smiley about?"

"I think I just set a date with Ethan."

Margot grinned. "So are you going to tell him how you feel?"

Chloe felt her cheeks heat. "Is it that obvious?"

"To me it is. But you're my favorite sister."

Chloe laughed. "I'm going to talk to him tonight and tell him how I feel." She pulled Margot's phone off the nightstand

and handed it to her. "And you're going to do the same with Owen. No more excuses. Tonight we lay it all on the line."

Margot sat up and took the phone hesitantly. She glanced up at Chloe. "Together?"

Chloe nodded. "Together."

33

Chloe

Chloe and Margot were seated on her bed watching the clock. It was after eleven. They'd heard their parents go to bed over an hour ago. *It was time.*

"Ready?" Chloe asked.

Margot let out a nervous breath and nodded. "As I'll ever be."

Chloe pulled her into a hug. "Good luck."

She picked up Darcy and quietly let herself out of her room to give her sister some space to talk to Owen. As Chloe made her way downstairs she repeatedly prayed Owen would take the news well. After the initial shock had worn off, Chloe couldn't imagine him not being excited. *Her sister was having Owen's baby! Their family was growing! She was going to be an aunt!*

Each thought released a euphoric burst of excitement that

tightened Chloe's chest. She knew this news would change Owen's plans and that being a parent was a huge responsibility, but she couldn't imagine him not wanting to do it. Especially after what Ethan told Chloe about their own lack of family.

And she'd seen the way Owen was with Margot. He looked at her like she was the sun, moon and stars. It was the same way her parents looked at each other. That had to be a good sign.

Chloe busied herself in the kitchen making hot cocoa and pulling out all the supplies for s'mores. She couldn't believe it was almost Christmas and she hadn't made s'mores once yet. Normally she made them every day during winter break. This had certainly been a different Christmas so far. But strangely, Chloe wouldn't change a thing about it.

Once she had everything she needed, she grabbed a treat for Darcy and tucked him in his fluffy argyle dog bed under the Christmas tree. She was so busy gazing at how cute he looked under the tree she almost didn't see Ethan until he was right next to her.

She grinned when she saw him. Tonight, it wasn't a surprise to find him in the living room with her at midnight. She'd asked him to meet her. "We've got to stop meeting like this," she said playfully.

Ethan snaked his hands around her waist and pulled her in close. "What if I don't want to?" he said softly, sending waves of nervous excitement though Chloe.

Her cheeks hurt with the intensity of her smile. "I don't want to either."

He kissed her beneath the twinkling lights that had been strung across the ceiling and Chloe felt her whole world narrow to nothing but Ethan. She could kiss him forever, but knowing they had much to discuss she forced herself to pull away.

"Come on, I have a surprise for you," she said taking his

hand and tugging him toward the pile of pillows and blankets she'd set up in front of the fire.

There were a million things she wanted to ask Ethan. Especially now that Margot was pregnant. Chloe knew she couldn't tell Ethan yet. But even without Margot's exciting news, there were still so many questions Chloe wanted answered. She wanted to know everything about Ethan. But more than that, she wanted to know how he felt about her.

Ethan

"What is all this?" Ethan asked as he watched Chloe settle into a nest of plaid pillows and fleece blankets in front of the fire.

She set up a tray spilling over with marshmallows, chocolate and graham crackers, along with dozens of types of candies and cookies. Next to the tray were two mugs of hot cocoa. As Ethan joined Chloe the enticing aroma of cinnamon made his stomach growl.

"It's your surprise," she said. "S'mores."

"I've never made s'mores," Ethan replied.

His answer made Chloe grin fiendishly for some reason. "I know."

"Oh yeah, and how's that?"

"I asked Margot. She said Owen had never made them so I figured you hadn't either."

He laughed. "Well, you figured right."

Chloe passed him his mug of cocoa. "First, you have to take a sip of this. It's my favorite kind."

"The horchata?" he asked.

Chloe's delicate eyebrows rose. "You remembered?"

Chloe, I memorize everything you say. He nodded and took a sip.

A moan escaped his lips after his first taste. The flavor was exquisite.

Chloe blushed. "Do you like it?"

"I think I love it." *Just like I think I love you, Chloe.* He certainly loved watching the effect he had on her. He linked his fingers with hers and let his thumb graze the back of her hand. In the firelight, her cheeks turned the color of ripe peaches.

"I can't believe you've never had s'mores before."

"Are you going to show me how to make them? Or just tease me about my insufficient knowledge of desserts?"

She grinned. "Okay," she said putting marshmallows onto skewers. She handed him one. "Just toast these in the fire and when you're done you put them between two graham crackers.

"That's it?"

"Well, normally, you put a piece of chocolate on the graham crackers but you can really use anything you want. I brought, cookies, peanut butter cups, chocolate cherries . . ."

Ethan couldn't help laughing at the excitement in Chloe's voice as she pointed out everything on her tray.

"What?"

"I have a feeling spending a lot of time with you might result in diabetes."

She shoved him playfully. "For your information I take health very seriously."

"I know. You're going to be a nurse."

Chloe

Chloe grinned. She loved that Ethan listened to her. They'd only briefly discussed that she was planning to go to school for nursing, but he remembered. She'd known Brady practically her whole life and he repeatedly asked her what major she was selecting when they'd been filling out college applications last year.

She smiled to herself and slowly shook her head, wondering how she'd ever thought getting dumped by Brady was the end of the world. *It was really just the beginning.*

It was Ethan's turn to question her. "What are you thinking?"

"Oh, just how some people fit together better than others."

Her comment seemed to amuse him, getting one of his rare half-smirks. "Are you talking about your terrible ex-boyfriend again, Chloe? Didn't I tell you to go easy on my ego?"

"I am talking about Brady, but what I'm trying to say is that he and I were never really a good fit. I couldn't see that before."

"But you see it now?" All joking had left Ethan's voice as he stared at her with his steady green eyes.

"Yes."

"But he clearly wants you back, Chloe."

"He told me as much. But I made it clear that it's not going to happen. I don't want to go backwards."

Ethan's voice was stained. "What do you want, Chloe?"

"I want to move forward. With you," she added in almost a whisper.

Ethan swallowed hard, his throat bobbing as he listened.

Chloe took a breath. "Ever since I met you, I've been seeing a lot of things differently."

"How so?"

"I think we're good for each other, Ethan," she said quietly. "I like talking to you. I like how you really listen to me. And I really like when you open up to me. I don't want it to end after Christmas."

. . .

Ethan

The only sound in the room was the *crackle-pop-hiss* of the fire and the pounding of Ethan's heart. *Are you saying what I think you're saying, Chloe?*

Did she actually feel what he felt? Did she want to be with him?

Ethan felt breathless as joy filled his chest so completely he had trouble finding his voice. He blinked at Chloe, consumed by hope as her words took an icepick to the last frozen layer of his heart.

Tonight when she'd rushed away from him at the party he'd been gripped by unrelenting fear. He knew in that moment that his heart belonged to her but he was so terrified to let it happen that he'd let his fear cripple him. He should have ran after her. He should have made Margot wait so he could tell Chloe everything in his heart.

After Chloe had texted Ethan, he did something so uncharacteristic that he felt obscenely foolish. On his way out the door he stopped at the wish station set up next to one of the many Christmas trees and scribbled a wish down on a slim strip of paper and tied it to the tree. 'Stop. Being. Afraid.'

They were only three little words, but they were the ones that had been holding him back his whole life. But not anymore. Not now, when he heard the words Chloe was saying.

'I think we're good for each other, Ethan.'

'I don't want this to end.'

He felt dizzy. *Don't say that, Chloe. Not unless you really mean it.*

But it was too late. His heart had heard every word and it was beating against his ribs so hard he was afraid it might claw its way out just to get to her.

"Chloe . . ." Ethan breathed.

"Oh, no!" Chloe jumped up and pulled his flaming marshmallow from the fire.

In the chaos of his overwhelming emotions, Ethan had forgotten about the skewer and it caught fire. It must've been hot when Chloe grabbed it because she immediately flung the skewer. The marshmallow stuck to the stone hearth and the flame flickered out harmlessly, but Chloe was sucking her fingers.

Ethan was at her side. "Are you okay?"

She laughed. "Fine. Nothing a little ice and honey can't fix."

34

Chloe

In the kitchen, Chloe could feel the heat of Ethan's eyes on her as she ran her hand under cold water for a few minutes and then grabbed an ice cube. She held the ice against her fingers. Only the first two had really gotten any sort of burn. It was mild, but she still rummaged around in the pantry for the raw honey. It was an amazing home remedy for burns.

She handed the jar to Ethan. "Can you open this for me?"

He twisted off the lid and followed her over to the sink, where she disposed of the half melted ice cube. She grabbed a spoon from the drawer and dipped it into the honey.

"If you put raw honey on a burn right after, it cuts down the healing time," she explained as he watched her cautiously.

"Does it hurt?" Ethan asked.

The pain in his eyes was so much worse than her burn that Chloe found herself wanting to comfort him. "No, Ethan. I'm fine, really. See?" She held up her sticky fingers for his inspection.

Ethan gently took her hand turning it over to inspect her fingers. His touch was so careful it sent shivers through her. His eyes met hers when his fingers met the honey. He pulled them through the sticky, sweet substance, gently massaging the honey into her scalded skin.

"Are you sure it doesn't hurt?" he asked.

It didn't hurt at all. Actually, the feel of his fingers sliding though the honey against her swollen skin was the exact opposite of painful. His touch was setting her heart on fire as the intensity of her desire grew. "It feels better now," she said, breathlessly.

Ethan pulled her hand slowly to his lips, pressing a light kiss to her finger tips. "How 'bout now?"

"Better," she whispered.

The corner of his lips tugged into that crooked grin that broke her heart and rebuilt it. He parted his lips and sucked one finger slowly into his mouth. "How 'bout now?"

Chloe's heart was in her throat. "Better."

He did it again. Each time he swirled his tongue around her fingertips, sucking the honey off in the most delicious way, until Chloe found her lips pressed to his, her still-sticky fingers in his hair.

The honey-sweet taste of his lips was like a drug and she couldn't get enough. Ethan swept her off her feet with frenzied passion. Chloe felt the counter under her as she wrapped her legs around Ethan's waist and clung to him for dear life. The way he kissed her made her feel like she was dying—dying in a fire of her own making, only to be reborn. Because nothing had ever been clearer; she was always meant to be his and he, hers.

ETHAN

. . .

THE LIGHTS FLICKERED on in the kitchen and Ethan pulled away from Chloe, startled by how caught up he was in the moment. Thank God it was Owen who'd walked in on them and not Chloe's parents. Ethan's shirt was off and Chloe's was nearly there, her bare stomach exposed. Ethan tugged her shirt down, putting himself between her and his brother to give her a moment to pull herself back together.

"Hey," Owen mumbled.

If he was startled to see them in the kitchen making out he didn't show it. He went straight to the fridge and grabbed a bottle of water. Ethan felt Chloe slide off the counter and join him. She discreetly handed him his shirt.

Owen stared at the water bottle for a moment, then he opened the fridge again and rummaged around in it for a minute. When he shut it his arms were full. Chloe laughed, and Owen gave her a strange look; half happy, half worried. "Margot's hungry," was all he said before he walked back out of the kitchen in a daze.

"That was weird," Ethan said, but when he looked at Chloe she had the most beautiful smile on her face. "What?"

"Nothing," she said, still grinning.

"What's going on? Does this have something to do with why Owen wasn't in bed when I snuck down here?"

"I'm not at liberty to say."

Ethan narrowed his eyes wondering what Chloe was keeping from him. "He's going to ask her to move in with him next semester."

Chloe's eyes grew so round he thought they might fall out. She looked like she might explode with delight as she bounced on her toes. "That's amazing!"

"You think so?"

"Absolutely! Don't you?"

"He sure seems excited about it."

"Are you?"

Ethan thought about it for a moment, but the answer came easily. "Yes. He deserves to be happy."

"So do you," Chloe said, taking his hand.

He squeezed it. *You certainly make me want to believe you, Chloe.* "So are you going to tell me what's going on with them or do I have to guess?"

Chloe led him back into the living room, shutting off the lights behind her. "You'll find out soon enough."

35

Chloe

THEIR SECOND ATTEMPT at making s'mores was much more successful. Mostly because Chloe didn't allow herself to touch Ethan. She was learning very quickly that it was easy to get carried away with him.

"So, what do you think?" she asked when Ethan polished off his peanut butter cup s'more.

"I can't believe I've been missing this all my life."

She laughed. "I told you." Chloe shook her head. "I still can't believe you survived nineteen years without experiencing this."

"I'm learning there's a lot I haven't experienced, Chloe."

"Well, you're going to have to make me a list so we can work on making you a well-rounded human."

He bunched his eyebrows together. "I'm well-rounded."

"No, you're stuffy. You grew up with a kitchen staff. I bet you even had a butler."

Ethan smirked and she knew she was right. He ate his last bit of s'more and lay down on his side, propping his head up on his fist. She loved how relaxed he looked lounging by the fire. The playful smirk on his face told her he was in a teasing mood and she was game for keeping things light.

"So, how many butlers are we talking?" she teased.

His face pinked. "Six."

"Six!"

"Shhh," he hissed shoving her knee. "It's not that big a deal. They're just like the concierges at your lodge."

"That's a hotel, Ethan. It's supposed to have staff," she replied. "Oh no, you're super rich, aren't you?"

He shook his head.

"Yes you are. You're a spoiled rich boy from Manhattan," she teased.

"No I'm not," he pulled her toward him, tickling her until she was breathless and snuggled against him.

"I can't believe I'm falling for a stuffy, rich kid from the city. I'm going to have to show you how to live, aren't I?"

He grinned. "I wouldn't say no to that."

She kissed his nose. "Good."

"Ya know, I don't think you're allowed to call me rich?"

"Why's that?"

"Have you forgotten I've seen that Christmas monstrosity you call a lodge? Your family seems to be doing pretty well for themselves."

"Yeah, they do alright." Chloe hugged a pillow and rolled onto her stomach.

"Can I ask you something?"

She nodded.

"Why do you guys live in this tiny little cabin when you have an amazing hotel right next door?"

She shrugged. “The lodge just opened a few years ago. Most of my life the family business was just the Christmas tree farm.”

“But things seem to be going well at the lodge.”

She nodded. “They are. I think my parents are just being cautious. Plus, my great-great-grandfather built this house. It has sentimental value.”

“I get that,” Ethan said pulling Chloe into his arms.

She sighed, loving the feel of having him so close. He undid the clip restraining her hair. It cascaded down around her shoulders and Ethan spent a few silent seconds just letting it slip through his fingers. Chloe could’ve laid there with him forever, nestled in his arms in front of the fire while he stroked her hair.

She didn’t think she’d ever felt so comfortable before. But as the silence stretched out she could almost feel the cloud of doubt settle over Ethan. She propped herself on her elbow to look at him and saw he was frowning.

“What’s wrong?”

“If I really were rich, would that change the way you feel about me?”

“Ethan, you already know how I feel about you.”

“Do I?”

“I thought I made it pretty clear in the kitchen.”

He smiled and tucked a strand of hair behind her ear. “You did, but I wouldn’t mind hearing you say it.” His sad eyes seemed to be saying, *I’ve been wrong before, Chloe.*

Ethan

Ethan gazed at Chloe trying not to need her confirmation. But he did.

I've been wrong before, Chloe. I need to hear it. Just once.

Ethan felt his chest tighten as he waited for Chloe's response. *Why had he just asked her to spell it out for him? What if she didn't tell him what he wanted to hear?* They'd only known each other for a few days. *What did he expect? A declaration of love?*

Chloe opened her mouth to respond and Ethan willed his ears not to listen. *Please don't break my heart, Chloe.*

"Ask me what my favorite Christmas memory is," she said.

Ethan blinked at her. That hadn't been the response he expected at all. *Did she not understand the question?* "You already told me. Ice skating with your family when you were nine or ten."

She grinned and sat up. "I love that you remember that. But I need to change my answer."

Ethan sat up, too. "Okay. What's your favorite Christmas memory?"

"This one, right now. Sitting in front of the fire with you, knowing that having you come into my life is the best Christmas gift I ever could've received. I don't think I'm falling for you, Ethan. I know I've fallen completely. And you make me never want to let go."

Ethan felt his chest tighten near bursting. He couldn't move. He couldn't breathe. But he didn't need to. Just like always, Chloe knew what he needed. She wrapped her arms around his neck and held him tight. His own arms responded naturally, crushing her to him.

He sucked in a deep breath as he buried his face in her neck, holding her tighter as his body began to shake with relief. He hadn't realized how terrified he was of losing this incredible girl who'd somehow stolen his heart until that exact moment when she told him she wanted him, too.

Chloe pulled back gently and brought her hand to his cheek to wipe away a tear he didn't even know he'd shed. "It's too soon to say it," she murmured. "But I feel it, Ethan." She pressed her hand to his heart. "And I don't ever want to lose this."

He nodded, afraid if he spoke he would shatter. But he knew she understood. *How could she not?* Her hand was directly over his pounding heart and he could see into her beautiful hazel eyes. Every thought of hers mirrored his own. *He loved her. He needed her. He never wanted to let her go.*

"I know you have to go back to Manhattan in a few days. But I'll be moving to the city for college in few months. Do you think . . ." Chloe looked down, her rare vulnerability showing.

Ethan stroked her petal-soft cheek. "What?"

Her eyes met his and the spark between them grew. "Do you think you could wait for me?"

Chloe

CHLOE WAS GREETED with the first full smile she'd ever gotten from Ethan and its sheer beauty was breathtaking. Her heart caught in her throat as he dazzled her with his grin. "Chloe, you have no idea how long I've waited for you. A few months longer is nothing."

Pure, unaltered joy coursed through Chloe's veins as Ethan pressed his lips to hers.

THE REST of the night was lost in a blur of blissful moments spent kissing beneath the fire's glow. Chloe didn't remember it burning out or when Ethan carried her to her bedroom, but she woke up in her room, wrapped in a blanket, with Darcy curled up at the foot of her bed. At first, she wasn't quite sure what had woken her, but then she saw Margot creeping into bed.

"Go-Go?" Chloe whispered, her voice heavy with sleep.

"Go back to bed," Margot whispered, kissing Chloe's forehead.

"Wait. Did you tell him?"

A huge smile lit up Margot's whole face. "I did."

"And?"

Margot climbed into bed with Chloe and snuggled up next to her. "And you were right. Everything is going to be okay. Actually, much better than okay."

Chloe sighed into her sister's arms. "I knew it," she whispered and then drifted back to sleep.

36

Ethan

THE SOUND of voices woke Ethan from his slumber. He was wrapped in a blanket snuggled on the leather couch in the Price's living room. Last night after tucking Chloe into bed, he'd returned to his room to find Margot and Owen sleeping together in Owen's bed. The moment seemed too peaceful and intimate to interrupt so Ethan had returned to the couch.

He'd been tempted to crawl into bed with Chloe, but Ethan didn't want to push his luck. He'd told her he'd wait for her and he'd meant it. Ethan knew that he wanted all of Chloe and that there was no need to rush. They would have plenty of time together once she moved to the city. *Maybe even a whole lifetime.*

The hope that filled him was a pleasant surprise. He wasn't used to waking up with a chest full of optimism. Ethan yawned, stretching as he sat up. He'd actually never slept better. After knowing this thing with him and Chloe wasn't one-sided he'd finally been able to silence the disquiet that had been growing in his newly exposed heart. When he finally focused on his surroundings, he was greeted with another pleasant surprise.

Chloe stood at the edge of the couch holding a mug of coffee. "Good morning, sleepyhead."

"Good morning, gorgeous," he said, pulling her onto his lap.

She giggled and let him nuzzle her neck while she carefully balanced the hot coffee.

The sound of Mr. Price clearing his throat brought Ethan back to reality. "Merry Christmas," he said, entering the living room followed by the rest of the family.

Chloe slid off Ethan's lap and took a seat next to him on the couch.

"Merry Christmas," Ethan replied.

"Okay, presents first or breakfast?" Mrs. Price asked as she bustled into the room carrying a tray of freshly baked cinnamon buns.

"Presents!" Margot exclaimed.

Ethan watched patiently while the Price family exchanged gifts. Surprisingly, they didn't buy a lot for each other. Ethan had remembered an abundance of extravagant gifts under the tree when his mother had been alive. But as he recalled, the gifts hadn't been what made Christmas feel special, it had been his mother who did that by the way she'd always made him feel loved.

As he watched Chloe's family together he realized it wasn't the gifts that made them so happy, it was this precious time they were spending together. Chloe opened a new stethoscope from her parents and squealed as she thanked them, telling them it was the exact one she'd wanted. *Of course it is, Chloe. They love you.*

Ethan found that thought warmed his heart. It made him happy that the girl he loved was so loved by others. He only hoped one day he would know her as well as her family did. That he would be able to read her mind and get her the exact things she wanted without her having to ask.

As the gift-giving started to wind to a close Ethan began to feel more apprehensive about his gift. Maybe he shouldn't give it to Chloe. He still had time to back out. No one would be any wiser. Well, Margot and Owen would, but they seemed so wrapped up in each other that they probably wouldn't notice if the roof caved in right now, let alone if Ethan bailed on his gift idea.

It had seemed so perfect when he thought of it yesterday . . . but maybe it was stupid. Chloe said she wanted to move forward and he had bought her a gift from the past.

Before he could think much more about it, Chloe bounded over to him, a shiny red box in her hands. "This is for you," she said, grinning.

"You got me something?"

"Of course."

Ethan tried to keep the shock from his face. It had been a long time since anyone had bought him a Christmas gift. He and Owen didn't exchange them. It didn't seem right given their feelings about the holiday. "Thank you."

"Don't thank me yet," Chloe said, teasingly.

Ethan unwrapped the box and pulled back the white tissue paper. When his fingers met the thick red wool and tiny bells his heart felt too big for his chest. *Chloe, you didn't.*

It was the sweater. The one from that first night in the kitchen. The one everyone in her family wore when they worked at the lodge. The same one that captured Everett's Christmas cheer.

"Welcome to the family," Chloe whispered as she placed a quick kiss on his cheek.

Ethan couldn't speak. Instead he yanked the sweater over his head and then pulled Chloe to her feet. "I have something for you, too. All of you actually," he said, speaking to her family.

Chloe

CHLOE FOLLOWED Ethan to the mudroom. She was about to ask him what he was doing when he opened the door and she saw six pairs of shiny new ice skates lined up in a row, each with a red velvet bow tied to the laces.

"Ethan!" She gasped. "Did you do this?"

"I wanted to make this your favorite Christmas."

She took his hands in hers as tears swam in her eyes. "It already is," she whispered. "Because I'm sharing it with you." Then she threw her arms around his neck and kissed him in front of everyone.

Ethan

AFTER ETHAN GOT over the shock of Chloe kissing him in front of her entire family, he managed to find his voice after clearing his throat several times. "I, um, got skates for everyone."

"Sweetheart, you didn't have to do that," Mrs. Price said.

"I know. But Chloe told me that her favorite Christmas was the one when you all skated on the frozen pond. When we took the snowmobiles out I noticed that it was frozen." He shrugged. "I thought maybe we could recreate a little Christmas magic."

Chloe's father looked at his daughter with pride. "I remember that year. You were ten. You spent more time on your rear end than your skates, baby girl. That was really your favorite Christmas?"

She nodded. "Absolutely. It was the last time we all took the entire day off to be together as a family."

Chloe's parents shared a look. Then her mother spoke. "Well, then I think we're well overdue for a family outing."

"What about the lodge?" Chloe asked.

"Family comes first," her mother replied without pause.

Chloe grinned and started passing out the skates. Ethan helped her, but when he handed Margot her pair, she frowned. It made Ethan pause. He knew he hadn't gotten her size wrong. Margot was the one he'd asked for the shoe sizes when he came up with the idea while picking up the ice sculpture with Owen.

"What's wrong?" Ethan asked her.

Margot reached for Owen's hand. He smiled at her and nodded. Margot swallowed hard and handed the skates back to Ethan. "I'm really sorry to ruin your incredibly sweet plans, Ethan. This was such a wonderful gesture, but I can't join you on the ice."

Chloe was suddenly by Ethan's side, looking concerned. She linked her fingers with his and mouthed, *'are you okay'* to her sister.

Margot nodded. But now everyone was looking at her. Owen squeezed Margot's shoulder and kissed her temple as he whispered something to her that no one else could hear.

"Why can't you join us?" Mr. Price asked.

Margot blew out a deep breath. "Because I'm pregnant."

Ethan felt his knees buckle. If he hadn't been holding Chloe's hand he was sure he would've stumbled, but she held him up. "What?" he whispered.

But Ethan's question was swallowed by the boom of Mr. Price's voice. It raised with each word he said, as did the red color of his face. "Excuse me? You're what?"

Mr. Price made to take a step toward Owen, but Mrs. Price stopped him.

"Tom," she said, placing a gentle hand on her husband's arm.

Again they shared a look and this one somehow took all the fight from Mr. Price. He ran a hand over his face, looking five years older when he was finished. He sagged back against the doorframe.

Mrs. Price walked across the room to her daughter.

"I'm sorry, Mom," Margot whimpered. "I know you didn't want this for me."

Mrs. Price frowned. "Margot, the only thing I've ever wanted for you is happiness."

Margot swallowed hard, swiping at her tears. She looked at Owen for a moment, then back at her mother. "I am happy, Mom. Happier than I've ever been."

"Then I'm happy, too." Mrs. Price opened her arms and Margot darted into them.

Ethan felt his heart crack wide open. What he wouldn't give to have a hug from his mother right now. There truly was nothing like family. But with that thought came a strange realization. Ethan's family was growing. His real family. His blood. He was going to be an uncle. He looked at Margot with fresh eyes, realizing she wasn't stealing Owen from him at all. She was giving Ethan more of Owen to love. *A nephew.*

He looked down at Chloe who was already smiling. "You knew."

It wasn't really a question but she answered anyway. "Since yesterday. I'm sorry I didn't tell you, but this was their news to share."

Ethan just stared at Chloe, shock and revelation making his heart pound so loud it drowned out the other conversation going on in the room.

"Are you mad?" Chloe asked.

"Mad?"

"That I didn't tell you?"

Ethan looked down at Chloe, a million happy thoughts exploding in his chest at once. *Chloe, I could never be mad at you. You're the best thing that's ever happened to me.*

"I am?"

Ethan was startled that she responded. But then he realized that he'd said his thoughts out loud for once and he couldn't stop the smile that slid into place. He pulled Chloe into his arms. "Absolutely. You, Margot, and your whole family. You have no idea what you've given me."

Chloe blinked up at him, reading the answer in his smile. But Ethan wanted to be sure she had no doubts. "You gave me somewhere I belong, Chloe. And I will always love you for that."

She grinned. "Good, because we're family now. And that's forever."

"Forever?"

She nodded.

He placed a gentle kiss on her lips. "I like the sound of that, Chloe."

She kissed him back. "Me too."

EPILOGUE

Chloe

CHLOE LACED UP HER SKATES, tugging to make sure they were tight.

"Quit stalling," Ethan teased, pulling her to her feet.

"I'm not," she argued. "I'm just taking it all in," Chloe said, looking over the perfect ice in awe. "I've wanted to do this for a very long time."

Ethan grinned. "Me too."

He held Chloe's hand tightly as she stepped onto the slick surface of the ice. At first she felt unsteady, but with Ethan by her side she knew she had nothing to fear. It had been that way ever since last Christmas.

Chloe could hardly believe another Christmas was just around the corner. She looked at the smiling faces of all the people on the ice at Rockefeller Center. The first snow of the season had just begun to fall. She couldn't believe she was actually here.

Ever since she was a little girl, Chloe had wanted to come ice skating in New York City. Now she was living here. She'd moved into an incredible apartment with Ethan, Margot and Owen. It was close to their campus. And she loved all of her classes. She even got to intern two days a week at a hospital. She was living her dream.

And if that weren't enough, she was dating her soulmate. She and Ethan had been dating since last Christmas and in that time, she'd seen him blossom into the most incredible man. Before him, she hadn't really known if she believed in miracles or a higher power, but now she did.

It had been an absolute Christmas miracle that blessed Chloe's family with the Hall brothers. She hated that it had taken them being abandoned by their birth family and adoptive family to bring them to hers. But she was glad for it, too. Because Chloe couldn't imagine her family without them.

Margot had given birth to a beautiful baby girl a few months ago and it had brought their already close family closer. And watching Ethan with his niece made Chloe fall in love with him all over again.

The broken boy she'd met almost a year ago was a ghost now, who rarely visited. Together, her family had helped Ethan grow into the strong, confident, caring man he was always meant to be.

After spending all of his school breaks helping Chloe and her family at the lodge, Ethan changed his major to hotel management. She loved watching him chat animatedly with her parents about ideas for their business. Sometimes, on days when Ethan was feeling even more joyful than usual, he talked about the future he wanted with her. *'Let's move back to Pine Island and have lots of kids. We can help your parents run the lodge and make them babysit so we can take the snowmobiles up to the ridge.'*

On days when he said things like that, Chloe thought her heart might burst. And she finally understood what her grandfather had meant about smiles ending famine. Because Ethan's now easy smile, would sustain her for a lifetime.

"What are you thinking?" he asked as they glided around the rink.

Chloe felt tears prick her eyes. "I'm thinking about how much I love you."

He gave her a breathtaking smile. "I love you more."

She shook her head. "Not possible."

Ethan turned his skates abruptly and skidded to a stop. Chloe laughed as he pulled her into his arms so swiftly she lost her balance. But not once did she worry he would drop her. She knew he never would. They were bookends, designed to hold each other up the way no one else could.

"So, what do you think?" he asked. "Was it worth the wait?"

"Rockefeller Center? Absolutely."

He gave her a crooked smile. "I'm glad you like it, but I was talking about us."

Chloe planted a sweet kiss on his lips. "Ethan, you are everything I hoped for and so much more. I'd wait for you forever."

He kissed her deeply before steadying her onto her feet. Then, with a smile bright enough to melt all the ice in New York City, he dropped to one knee and pulled a ring from his pocket. "Waiting is overrated."

To my readers,

I want to personally thank you for taking the time to seek out this great little indie book. Writing is truly my passion. I believe each of us can find a small part of ourselves in every book we read, and carry it with us, shaping our world, our adventures and our dreams.

Following my dream to write frees my soul but knowing others find joy in my writing is indescribable. So thank you for your support and I hope your enjoyed your brief escape into the magic of these pages.

If you enjoyed this story, don't worry, there's plenty more currently rattling around in my rambunctious imagination. Let me and others know your thoughts by sharing a review of this book. Reviews help shape my next writing projects. So if you want more books like this one be sure to shout it from the rooftops (or social media.) ;-)

- Christina Benjamin

PLEASE LEAVE A REVIEW HERE

ACKNOWLEDGMENTS

I'd like to thank everyone who made this book possible.

To my husband, whose unyielding belief and encouragement forces me to pour my best self onto each and every page, and to all the time and effort he dedicates to making my musing into actual tangible dreams.

To Molly and Megan, who always say yes when I hand them yet another pile of pages.

To Vince for literally sitting by my side during every word, edit and rewrite. You helped breathe life and authenticity into Darcy and every pet I write. You are the stinky heartbeat at my feet and I wouldn't trade you for the world.

To all the strange places I lock myself away to write, to Nancy, my write-or-die girl, and to my NINC guys for challenging my writing sprints to reach new limits.

To New York City, for all the wonderful memories I acquired on each childhood visit. There is truly something magic there, especially around Christmas time.

To my little brother, who loves a good snowball fight and anything chocolate. Thank you for showing me how awesome it is to have a little brother to plot and laugh with.

A huge thank you to my parents for giving me a childhood in the northeast, surrounded by snow, sleigh rides, frozen cheeks, hot cocoa and real Christmas trees—even if we had to dig them up ourselves. Thank you for teaching me to believe in the magic of Christmas, look for everyday miracles and the people who need them most, and best of all thank you for teaching me that love conquers all.

Lastly, thank you to all of you who are taking the time to read this to the very end. I hope your holiday is merry and bright and full of the magic of Christmas.

ALSO BY CHRISTINA BENJAMIN

YOUNG ADULT CONTEMPORARY ROMANCE

(All Boyfriend Books are Stand-Alone Novels and can be read in Any Order)

The Practice Boyfriend (Book 1)

The Almost Boyfriend (Book 2)

The Goodbye Boyfriend (Book 3)

The Holiday Boyfriend (Book 4)

The Stand-In Boyfriend (Book 5)

The Maybe Boyfriend (Book 6)

The Accidental Boyfriend (Book 7)

The Summer Boyfriend (Book 8)

The Wedding Boyfriend (Book 9)

The Winter Boyfriend (Book 10)

To my readers,

I want to personally thank you for taking the time to seek out this great little indie book. Writing is truly my passion. I believe each of us can find a small part of ourselves in every book we read, and carry it with us, shaping our world, our adventures and our dreams.

Following my dream to write frees my soul but knowing others find joy in my writing is indescribable. So thank you for your support and I hope your enjoyed your brief escape into the magic of these pages.

If you enjoyed this story, don't worry, there's plenty more currently rattling around in my rambunctious imagination. Let me and others know your thoughts by sharing a review of this book. Reviews help shape my next writing projects. So if you want more books like this one be sure to shout it from the rooftops (or social media) ;-)

ABOUT THE AUTHOR

Award-Winning author, Christina Benjamin, lives in Florida with her husband, and character inspiring pets, where she spends her free time working on her books and enjoying a macaron with a glass of wine.

Christina is best known for her bestselling Young Adult romance novels, The Boyfriend series. The Boyfriend series proves that book boyfriends are like Chocolate… you can never have enough. Check out the Boyfriend series for fast, fun, YA romance reads. These stand alone novels let you fall in love with new characters every time.

Want to talk books with Christina? Join her super secret Facebook group Words & Wine with Christina Benjamin, where she'll answer questions and discuss upcoming novels with her readers.

To learn about new books and more fun stuff, follow her at:

FACEBOOK
@ChristinaBenjaminAuthor

TWITTER
@authorcbenjamin

INSTAGRAM
@authorcbenjamin

PINTEREST
@authorcbenjamin

WEBSITE
www.christinabenjaminauthor.com

www.ingramcontent.com/pod-product-compliance
Lightning Source LLC
Chambersburg PA
CBHW030529310726
48979CB00010B/1846/J

* 9 7 8 1 7 3 2 6 1 2 3 2 7 *